Also by
Jeannette de Beauvoir

Mysteries:
Sydney Riley series:
Death of a Bear
Murder at Fantasia Fair
The Deadliest Blessing
A Killer Carnival
A Fatal Folly
The Matinée Murders
Martine LeDuc series:
Deadly Jewels
Asylum
Trinity Pierce series:
Murder Most Academic (as Alicia Stone)

Historical Fiction:
Our Lady of the Dunes
Lethal Alliances

The Lethal Legacy

A Provincetown Mystery

Jeannette de Beauvoir

The Lethal Legacy: A Provincetown Mystery
Copyright © 2020 by Jeannette de Beauvoir

Published by HomePort Press
PO Box 1508
Provincetown, MA 02657
www.HomePortPress.com

ISBN   978-1-7340533-5-7
eISBN 978-1-7340533-6-4

Cover Design by Miladinka Milic

1

It all started with a disappearance.

    Two disappearances, in fact, that you'd think were completely unrelated. But I'm starting to think life doesn't work that way. We put ideas and people and situations neatly into boxes, but they're wild, aren't they: they won't stay where we put them, they won't stay separate. There's an undercurrent of connectedness flowing just under the surface of every event, every interaction, just waiting to bubble up and be noticed.

    The first disappearance was in 1620. A ship called the Mayflower had sailed from Europe and was safely at anchor in Provincetown Harbor on a sunny afternoon when Dorothy May Bradford inexplicably tumbled off the deck and drowned.

The second disappearance took place on a dark night in 1851, when an escaped slave who went only by the name of Sarah also inexplicably fell, she from a fishing-boat well out into Cape Cod Bay, and disappeared under the waves.

There have been disappearances since those two, of course. Mostly in the spring, which has long baffled me: our winters are windblown and lonely, but spring arrives in fits and starts with so much promise of better times you'd think people would stick around.

Still, these two first disappearances, of historical interest only, stitched together a story that ended up not in a disappearance—but in murder.

***

It was a perfect fall day, and murder was the last thing on my mind.

The Race Point Inn, where I work, was bustling, and I was at the center of the bustle. I'm the inn's wedding organizer, and we were gearing up for no fewer than twelve weddings in the space of a single October week.

That week was Women's Week, the longest-running lesbian event in the northeast, bringing thousands of women—young, old, in couples or alone-yet-hopeful— to Province-town. There are over three hundred events, activities, workshops, performances, dances… the list goes on. A few of the activities and two of the workshops were scheduled to take place at the inn.

Mostly, though, for us, the week was about the weddings.

A while back and for a couple of years, two enterprising inn owners created an event they called Bride Pride—a one-day mass wedding mildly reminiscent, truth be told, of the Moon Unification Church weddings—which was held first at Roux, the women's inn, and then up at the Pilgrim Monument on High Pole Hill, with a spectacular view of the harbor and the town. Weddings, renewals of vows, that sort of thing. Music; food; local celebrity Kate Clinton officiant-for-the-day.

It didn't last; the founders sold up and moved away, and no one else seemed to want to take on what was surely a logistical nightmare.

But women still want to tie the knot here in P'town—Massachusetts, after all, led the way in the legalization of same-sex marriage— and while I'm not particularly interested in organizing mass ceremonies, I *had* managed to schedule twelve individual ones. My bosses, Glenn (the inn's owner) and Mike (the inn's manager) were ecstatic and thought it was the best thing to happen to us all year; my boy-friend Ali thought I was insane.

All of them were, of course, correct.

I was wrangling florists, wedding offici-ants, photographers, and musicians. The food was, blessedly enough, not my domain: that was down to Adrienne, the inn's diva chef, who kept the restaurant in its Michelin four stars and ruled the kitchen with an iron fist and the occasional flinging of cutlery. The couples were all staying at the inn and running into each other as the week began, building a level of excitement that was palpable. Friday and Saturday had already been jam-packed with ac-tivities for participants—whale-watching, tea dance, sunset cruises and stand-up comedy—and by late Monday I'd ticked four of my scheduled weddings off the list.

"Take your vitamins," counseled Ali on the telephone. He lives in Boston, two and a half hours' drive—or ferry—from P'town. "You know you always forget to take them."

"You sound like my mother," I complained. Well, like my mother would sound if she were a normal mother.

Ali knows that. "Someone's got to," he said.

"You sure you can't come down and keep me company?" I knew the answer, but it was worth asking the question anyway. Hope springs eternal and all that jazz.

"Not a chance, *cara*." Ali is Lebanese-American, but his Italian is fluent and he thinks it's sexy. He's right. "We're in the middle of something here."

I didn't ask what it was; most of what Ali does is pretty hush-hush. He works for Immigration and Customs Enforcement, in the human-trafficking division. A great deal of ICE seems to be about getting people out of the country; Ali's department makes sure the ones who are here actually *want* to be.

"Anyway," he was saying, "you'll be too busy to notice whether I'm there or not. You know how you get."

I sighed. He was right. I knew how I got. "I'll remember to take my vitamins," I said in resignation.

"*Quello è buono.*" He must be missing me; I didn't usually get full sentences in Italian. "Have you seen Mirela?"

"Yesterday." Mirela is my best friend and, surprisingly enough, Ali's as well. She's a successful and brilliant painter who came to Provincetown years ago as part of the influx of Bulgarian students who arrive every summer to work three or four jobs and keep the tourist town running. Mirela fell in love with Provincetown, Provincetown fell in love with Mirela's art, and she's been here ever since. She is blonde and beautiful and I couldn't imagine the place without her. She just fit in.

There'd been a hiccup back in the spring when her sister had given birth to an unwanted daughter and Mirela had gone to Plovdiv—to everyone's surprise—to adopt the baby. We'd been more than a little worried about her staying in Bulgaria, but she'd come back home, tiny Liliana (Lily for short) in tow, and had been making a credible effort since then at being an artist and a mother at the same time. I didn't envy her. I have a theory that either you're born with a maternal instinct or you're not, and I couldn't find even a hint of it in myself. Lily might be interesting once she hit, oh, maybe eleven; at the moment she didn't really have much to offer in the personality department.

Ali, on the other hand, was fascinated. Partly because Mirela had quietly assumed he'd be godfather, and partly just because he simply (and, to me, inexplicably) found Lily appealing. "You can't be godfather," I'd pointed out when he told me what Mirela had asked for.

"Why not?" He knew why not; he was goading me.

"What does Islam say about it?"

"Funny you should ask," he'd said. "I posed the same question to my parents' imam."

"And?"

"If it were a religious thing, then of course I couldn't," he said. "But Mirela's as lapsed an Eastern Orthodox Christian as you can find. She wants us just for Lily's future and well-being. Purely secular. So I said yes."

Us. There was that word. I don't generally mind being grouped with Ali. But playing godmother to his godfather? It conjured up other things that couples do, like live together or get married, neither of which idea I wanted to entertain. I wasn't even sure about how *I* felt about being a godmother—I'm pretty lapsed, as Catholics go—but of course I said yes, too;

I could hardly do anything else. For Mirela. All in all, it was going to be an interesting time.

Now I said, "She's got someone coming in to look after Lily a couple of afternoons so she can go to her studio. She's pleased about that."

"Good for her. And what about you?"

"Me? No, I don't have anyone coming in a couple of afternoons to look after me."

He actually laughed. "Are you pleased with Women's Week this year?"

I smiled; I couldn't help it. "It's fantastic," I said.

Well, it turned out I was right. But only in a way.

2

Women's Week starts on the weekend, but its real centerpiece is on Tuesday evening, the Women's Community Dinner. I usually try to go; it's good PR for us, and I never know who I might meet who'd want to come back the next year for a wedding or event, or just to stay at the Race Point Inn.

Plus, it's just fun.

The dinner, as it's known, is held out at the Provincetown Inn, on the opposite end of town from the Race Point, way out in the West End by the breakwater. That's the start of Commercial Street, in fact: the inn is number one.

Across the street is the old Murchison estate, perching high on a hill overlooking the tidal marsh, now divided up into plots with mostly ultra-modern houses on them, glass and chrome and concrete and teak. I knew the property too well. Once upon a Bear Week, I'd been up at the contemporary mansion (once the residence of a well-known psychologist called Carl Murchison, hence the name) that sits highest up on the hill with a spectacular view of Land's End, but hidden from the eyes of curious onlookers by a thicket of shrubs and trees. Just as a matter of interest, the house—known as the Gropius House, since it was designed by Walter Gropius's firm at a cost of three hundred thousand dollars, a princely sum at the time—had been named one of the best-designed homes in 1959 by *Architectural Record* magazine.

I'd almost been killed there.

I always turn my back a little resolutely at that particular corner and focus instead on the Provincetown Inn, which doesn't have the refined expensive allure of the houses across the way on the Murchison estate; instead, it's approachable, slightly shabby, and welcoming. It's an amazing place for a whole lot of reasons. One, because in space-starved Provincetown, it's huge, with wings all over the place and an outside pool and a tremendous expanse of lawn, all overlooking the harbor and Long Point. Two, because the inside hallways and lobbies are all made to look like outdoor street scenes from the 1800s, with mural after mural on the walls everywhere you look. The story about the murals is that sometime in the 1960s an artist called Don Aikens came to spend the summer and, having no money, offered to paint the walls for the price of a room for the season, using old postcards as his models.

In a town where gentrification often seems intent on erasing anything quaint and curious, those murals are a treasure.

Large round tables are set up in one of the function rooms—and it's all lovely and elegant, linen tablecloths and napkins—with a buffet and cash bar adjoining, and the food is moderately good. Not to Adrienne the diva chef's level of good; not even to the Mews or Mistralino's or even Mirela's favorite Ciro and Sal's level of good; but not to be sneezed at, either. You pay a fee when you sign up for the dinner, but once you're there all you have to do is pay for drinks, and as my friend Pat who drives the tourist trolley said, "Lesbians love free food."

"It isn't free," I pointed out.

"It might as well be," she said. "They paid for it months back. It feels free. That's all that matters."

There's free entertainment, too, as every musician or comedian who's performing during Women's Week gives a sample of what she has on offer, in the hopes that everyone at the dinner will come buy tickets and see the show. It works; they do. Let's face it: the shows—whether music, comedy, or drag—are a draw for any of P'town's theme weeks.

The evening is emceed by Char Priolo, who once had a band called The Dyketones back in the day (way before my time, I should add) and is generally recognized as one of Provincetown's Personalities with a capital P. At some point in the evening there's an award presented to the Woman of the Year.

Seats are reserved in advance, with groups of women who see each other at the event every year commandeering whole tables. "Pods of lesbians," as Pat calls them. "Lesbians always travel in clusters," she said. They certainly did during Women's Week.

I called Mirela. "Are you going to the dinner?"

"Do not be ridiculous, sunshine." Mirela thinks "sunshine" is a term of endearment; I'd never pointed out its more frequent ironic usage to her.

"I'm not being ridiculous. You went last year."

An exaggerated sigh. "I went the year before last," she said, as though anyone in their right mind should have that fact at their fingertips, "as the guest of a client."

"What, so you're waiting for another client to invite you?" Mirela makes roughly eight times more money than I do. "You could afford to go."

"I have Lily."

"You could afford a babysitter." I was seriously going to have to start dealing with my jealousy of a six-month-old.

"Sunshine. Go to your dinner."

I growled some more, but Mirela with her mind made up is unmovable. Not that I minded so much going alone—at the very least, I'd be seeing "my" wedding couples there, and other women who were staying at the inn; and anyway I spend a lot of time doing things on my own, I keep myself good company.

I did a little prep work—I may not be into the high-maintenance decades of life yet, but as my thirties tick by I'm aware of them lurking in my future—by tying my long red hair into something approximating a chignon, doing the

13

eyeliner-mascara-lipstick routine, and choosing a decent dress to wear. Mission accomplished.

I might not mind being alone, but it's nice to have a friend, too, so when I got to the Provincetown Inn and looked around for someone I knew, I was delighted to latch onto my primary-care doctor. "Thea!"

Thea looked pleased to see me, which was nice, and grabbed my arm without thinking, which was a lot less nice. She's my doctor, so she should have known better: I'd broken my arm back in June, and while the surgeon was contented with my range-of-motion progress, I was still going to physical therapy, and I still had pain.

Specifically, right where Thea had just grabbed me.

She was oblivious. "Sydney! How perfect to see you! I've been meaning to call, but you know, the summer…"

I knew. Provincetown is a summer resort town; most of us make our livings, in one way or another, from the tourist trade. Which in essence means often working two or three jobs in the summer and surviving unemployment the rest of the year. Winters we dig in and take care of each other; summers we're lucky if we see each other in passing.

She hugged me, a small, African-American woman with the biggest, darkest, most beautiful eyes I'd ever seen on anyone, a great doctor and a greater friend. We usually rented a small sailboat from Flyer's a couple of times a summer and took it out careening around the harbor; somehow this summer had slipped away and we'd only done it once, back in May, before the film festival where I'd broken my arm. I should have probably made the time—for that and about half a dozen other things. Then again, my arm had been immobilized for a while; maybe it wouldn't have been such a brilliant idea. "Everything good with you?" I asked.

She nodded, vigorously—everything Thea does is at a hundred miles per hour. "Where are you sitting? And do you *have* to sit there? It's just, listen, there's an extra place at my table, Karen Porter isn't here, she had to work unexpectedly after all and isn't getting in to town until tomorrow, and it would be just *perfect* to have you join us!"

I had no idea who Karen Porter was. "I'd love to," I said. I didn't know where my seat was, but surely I wouldn't be missed—and I had in fact missed seeing Thea.

After a fair bit of milling around—organizing drinks, getting food from the buffet, listening to the welcome speech—I settled in, Thea on one side of me and a woman wearing a caftan on my left. "I'm Sydney," I said to her, holding out my hand.

"Regina."

"That's a beautiful name!" I exclaimed.

She laughed, her voice rich and musical. "Everyone says so," she said. "But, actually, sorry, most people call me Reggie." She touched the arm of the person next to her, an attractive woman with straightened black hair and skin the color of crème caramel. "This is Jordan," she said. "Honey, this is Sydney."

We did the nodding-the-head thing one does at big banquet tables and for a few minutes everyone attended to their food. But I'm in the hospitality industry, and I have—as anyone who knows me would be happy to tell you—a big mouth, so I didn't waste any time getting into hospitable mode. "Is this your first time in P'town?" I asked.

Reggie nodded. "Believe it or not, yeah. Jordan's been performing all over Canada at women's events, but we've never come here.

We talked about doing it but never got around to it." She smiled and shrugged. "So much to do at home, yeah? But then, this year, Jordan has this project she wanted to come to Provincetown for. So it was easy for her manager to arrange for her to perform this week."

I looked at Jordan. "You're part of the show tonight?"

She nodded, swallowing whatever she'd just bitten into and taking a quick sip of water. "Tonight, yes, and I'm singing at the Crown & Anchor all week, eh?" She had that Canadian habit of making a lot of her sentences sound like questions, inviting agreement.

"What kind of music do you do?"

She smiled. "Jazz, blues, torch songs, a little of everything."

"I can't wait to hear you." And I couldn't; the performers who put on shows during Women's Week are good—some are even great, don't get me wrong; but it's almost always the usual suspects, year after year, coming in the summer and leaving in the fall, heading out to do the Olivia cruises, returning to town for this one week in October before leaving to work warmer resort venues in the winter. I loved them all, but it would be a breath of fresh air to hear someone new, too.

Then I remembered the rest of what Reggie'd said. "What's the project?"

Thea was clearly following the conversation. She touched my arm. "Wait until you hear about this," she said, nodding vigorously, the beads in her hair clacking together. She sounded excited.

"You all know each other?" Making the assumption they were together since they were all Black seemed a little racist. I'm working on actually thinking *before* I open my mouth.

Some days I'm more successful than others.

Reggie smiled. "Thea and I met in medical school," she said. "We go way back, don't we?"

Thea giggled. She's a giggler. "Not *that* far back," she said. "You make us sound ancient! Besides, we were a lot more serious then. I feel younger now than I did in school, can you believe that?"

Reggie pushed her chair back a bit from the table to reveal her footwear: Chuck Taylor high-tops in streaky rainbows. "Really, Thea? We were more serious then? Back in medical school? Don't you remember these shoes?"

"Those aren't the same ones!" Thea protested, still laughing, "They couldn't be!" She turned to me and said, "We all wore our shoes out, back then, doing internships and residencies. It takes a toll on your feet. Reggie's high-tops were famous. I think she went through a dozen pairs."

"And they always made you smile," Reggie reminded her.

"Even when we were all trying to be serious young doctors, Reggie always reminded us to not leave the humor out of the equation," said Thea. "It taught me a lot."

I took a sip of wine. "So what's this project?" I asked, as Reggie slid her chair back up to the table. I said directly to Jordan, "Depending on what you're doing, I know a lot of people in town, maybe I can help. I can introduce you to anyone, if you'd like."

Jordan shook her head. "I don't think so, but thank you." She sipped her own cocktail. "So what I'm doing, it's really cliché," she said. I was finding the lilt in her voice charming. "So don't laugh. But I'm tracing my roots. My family. All that."

"Nothing funny about that." If I were to trace my own roots, it would only be in the desperate hope I'd find I'd been adopted. "And it led you to Provincetown?"

She was finishing off her food, nodding. "Right," she said. "We're Canadian. We both grew up in Halifax. That's in Nova Scotia," she added, kindly, in case I didn't know. Canadians are like that: helpful. "My great-great-grand-mother was a house slave on a plantation down in Virginia. And she was literate," she said. "I think that was a big thing, back then. Not a lot of people were. She wrote a lot—letters, journals, lists, she even wrote a couple of short stories. All of it once she'd escaped, of course, once she was in Halifax. Memoirs, I guess you'd call them. Short bits and bobs. Her son kept them all and passed them on—to his daughter and her husband, they were my grandparents. After my parents died, I got in-terested in my family history, and I was lucky to have a lot of material to start with."

"Sounds fascinating," I said. My mother writes nothing but cranky letters to the editor and snarky comments on blogs. A lot of them.

"She—that's my great-great-grandmother, her name was Callie—had been reasonably well treated, whatever that means in the con-text. That's why she could read and write. Ap-parently she was expected to read to a member of the plantation owner's family, who was blind. But then she and her sister Sarah managed to escape, and they used the Underground Railroad to get smuggled north."

That was certainly intriguing. I wondered if she planned to write a book about her ancestor's story. Sounded like a bestseller to me.

Thea said, "But it was a bad time to do it." She obviously knew what came next in the narrative.

"Why?" I asked.

"Slaves used to be able to come north and live in places like Philadelphia and Boston," Thea said. "Up until 1850."

Jordan nodded. "The Fugitive Slave Act," she said. "It meant that slave-hunters could go up north to Philadelphia and New York and Boston, or anywhere in fact, and recapture any escaped slaves. Even if they were north of the Mason-Dixon Line, which used to be the boundary. So no one was really safe anywhere anymore."

I was still waiting for the P'town connection. "So what did they do? Your ancestor and her sister, I mean?"

"They were brought out here," said Jordan, a gleam in her eye. She'd sensed my impatience. "Didn't you know? Provincetown was a stop on the Railroad."

"You're kidding!" She had to be. We're at land's end, here. There isn't anything else beyond us; there's nowhere to go. Travel east from Provincetown and the first landmass you'll hit is Portugal. The bartender, I concluded, must have been making extra-strong cocktails. "Why?" It sounded pretty dead-end to me, the only advantage—*maybe*, and even that was a stretch—being it was so far off the beaten trail that it might not be worth the effort to chase anyone out here.

"They really did use railroad language," Jordan was saying in response to Thea, some remark or question I'd missed. Beside her, Reggie got up to refill her plate. "Anyone want anything?"

We all shook our heads; I was entranced. "Like what?"

"People called stationmasters or ticket masters ran the homes and businesses where slaves could rest and eat," said Jordan. "Those places were called stations and depots. Goods and money were contributed by people called stockholders, and the conductors were responsible for moving fugitives from one station to the next along the network." She took a deep breath. "Anyway, apparently there were some stations here in P'town, three or four of them. At least, that's what she wrote about, and so I wanted to come in person to see it."

"But why P'town? I still don't get it," I said. I couldn't see what I was missing.

Thea was grinning. "The conductors around here," she said, carefully weighting the words for meaning, "were fishermen."

Jordan smiled; my face must have been registering sudden comprehension. She said, "Fishing boats from Provincetown went out to George's Bank and met up with fishing boats from Nova Scotia. And that wasn't anything out of the ordinary. For centuries, ship's logs showed them meeting at sea, there was an established tradition of exchanging mail and goods. Why not people?"

Thea said, "Two of the original members of the Anti-Slavery Society in P'town were members of a family of ship captains originally from Nova Scotia, who'd settled in Provincetown. There was a strong connection there already. So why not use that route for the Railroad?"

I shivered at the image their words conjured, the waves first lifting the boats high and then dropping them down into the troughs, no moon to see by—they'd have been as careful as the local mooncussers about making sure the night was dark enough so they wouldn't be seen—the wind and the cold. We weren't talking small boats, either, not in those days: those were the Grand Banks schooners. I knew what they looked like; we had a half-scale model of one of them, the *Rose Dorothea*, in the library. Half-scale was *huge*.

They'd need to lower lifeboats to transfer the passengers, of course, unless they set up a breeches buoy. Holding the dinghies together to get shivering, exhausted people from one to the other; a different kind of smuggling. Threats from the pursuers, from the weather, from the sea itself. "But that must have been extraordinarily dangerous!" I exclaimed.

"It was. In fact, Callie's sister, Sarah, went over the side; she didn't make it," said Jordan soberly. "But Callie did, and she settled in a part of Halifax, well, a separate little village really, that was called Africville."

"Jesus," I said.

She raised her eyebrows. "The name? Yeah, it was racist, and the place has its own sordid history, places like that usually do. My family were extremely poor for generations. But," she paused, "they were *free*."

It was a moving story, and I found I had a lot of questions bubbling up. *Why didn't Sarah make it? What became of Callie in the new land? What was life like in Africville? How had Jordan traced it all?* But Char was up tapping on the microphone and the evening was getting ready to start in earnest.

I slipped over to the bar to secure a second glass of Côtes du Rhône from the laconic bartender, some kid I didn't know, and got back to my seat just in time for the first comedian, Poppy Champlin—who was coincidentally enough another Canadian. It seemed to be the night for northern performers.

Poppy was still doing her thing at the microphone when a manager came over to our table and said something in Thea's ear. She nodded as he hurried away and she put her napkin on the table. "Gotta go," she said, her voice low so as not to detract from Poppy's lines.

"What's going on?"

"Nothing much. Nothing to worry about. A guest just turned her ankle out in the lobby. I'll be back in five."

Poppy was funny, and got a lot of applause when her bit was finished. Char got up on stage and thanked her, then turned to the audience. "I'm told to ask if there's a doctor here?" she said, looking around the tables. "One of the staff cut themselves."

Reggie raised her hand, already out of her seat. Mishap City tonight, I thought. Jordan and I exchanged smiles and shrugs as Char introduced Zoe Lewis.

I'd eaten far too much, and the wine was making me sleepy. I decided to wait until after Jordan's turn at the microphone and after Thea got back, and then head home. My cat Ibsen was going to be watching the clock for sure, since he gets special treats every evening when I give him his thyroid pill—and, besides, I had a wedding in the morning. Better to be rested for all the things that, naturally, were going to go wrong. I listened to Zoe—I really love listening to Zoe, she has the warmest happiest presence of anyone I've ever met—doing her one-woman-band thing, and then another comedian I didn't know but who was howlingly funny, before Jordan was announced.

I might never have heard of her, but these women certainly had; the applause was warm and welcoming.

She had a male keyboardist I recognized right away: Jon Richardson, who does piano bars at a couple of places in town, Tin Pan Alley and the Crown & Anchor, and who's also a singer-songwriter who records with another local musician, Peter Donnelly. I like Jon. He's self-deprecating and funny and has been playing piano since he was born, or something like that. He sat down, looking a little bemused— maybe he wasn't used to being around so many women in one room—while Jordan, at the microphone, thanked the organizers for inviting her. She was twice interrupted by hooting. Okay, why was I the only one in the room who hadn't heard of this woman?

She glanced at Jon and he gave her a couple of gentle opening chords and she started singing and the room fell quiet as though mesmerized.

It was a popular song, but no one had ever sung it like this. Jordan sang with nuance and passion and melody and truth. Her tone carried the chords of memory the way the wind makes magical scents fly.

> *Who we mean to be*
> *Should be more real than*
> *Anything we are now…*

It was the kind of moment that seizes you, that makes you want to go out and do something good, create something beautiful, believe that there's hope for the future. Hell, yes, let's be who we mean to be.

Eyes already set
on a land we never dreamed of
Moving closer every day

Jordan's voice was pure and clear, passion running through it like a swirl of froth on a cappuccino. I could almost believe myself to be one of the dreamers. I was moving closer to that land.

Come take my hand, for hope
is an unturned page in a book
That we're all still writing…

I looked around me; everyone was rapt, shocked almost, as if collectively holding their breath.

It lasted until three full beats after she finished and would have lasted longer if someone hadn't started screaming right outside the door to the back patio.

3

It was Margaret Green, one of the smokers, who'd gone out to have a quick cigarette and saw the foot protruding from the bushes nearby. It was dark, by now, but there were motion-activated lights out there and she'd activated them.

Everyone of course did the worst thing possible and crowded over to the door and the big plate-glass window to see what was happening. I looked around, but Thea and Reggie were both gone and Jordan was still on the stage, unwilling to step down into what was quickly becoming a mêlée. She was still holding the microphone and looking a little lost.

"Coming through!" I recognized the voice: Julie Agassi, sometimes-friend and the head of the detective section of the Provincetown Police Department. I hadn't seen her, but she'd no doubt been attending the dinner; as she pushed through now I saw she was wearing civvies. "Move, please." The voice got louder. "Provincetown police! Make way!"

That did it. The parting of the Red Sea unfolded and I took advantage of it by following close behind her. Not that I'm one for rubbernecking, but everything that happens in this tourist town affects all of us, and the more I knew, the better prepared I'd be for any fallout that could possibly affect the Race Point Inn. Had one of the guests gotten tipsy and fallen into the pool—or the harbor? Had someone—

It was a shoe. The shoe was attached to a leg, and the leg was protruding from the bushes strategically arranged around the outside of the inn. And I realized with a cold feeling in the pit of my stomach that I'd been sitting next to those shoes only a short while before. *Breathe, Riley, just breathe...*

Julie had her mobile phone out and was speaking tersely into it, while at the same time making sweeping gestures to get women to back off. She turned around and saw me. "Riley," she hissed. "Help out here, will you?"

It was a pleasant change from Julie's usual reaction to seeing me, which is, generally speaking, a mixture of resignation and suspicion. It would be good to live up to the change. I was standing still in shock; I shook myself, mentally, and brought my voice up to wedding-wrangling volume. "Back up, everyone, please. Let the police do their job. Everybody, back in the dining room!"

An amazing number of the bystanders obeyed; can't say we're not polite. The assistant manager from the inn came hurrying out, wringing his hands; I don't think I'd actually ever seen anyone do that before. "Officer—"

"Detective," Julie corrected crisply. She was still on the phone. "Woman is unresponsive, possible suspicious death," she said into it. She squatted down and held her flashlight onto the body, and I'd been right: it was Reggie. Those rainbow high-tops were unmistakable.

That she was a body was clear. For reasons beyond my understanding, I have significantly more experience with dead bodies than do most people. As Julie would have said, I wasn't most people. She often blames me for finding them. When, in truth, on more than one occasion, I've come close to *being* one.

In any case, unresponsive was definitely how I'd have described Reggie. Everyone checks, of course, but when a soul has left a body, you know it. You feel it. There's an emptiness that's hard to describe but that's almost palpable.

Time to tell Julie the bad news. *Breathe, Riley: just breathe.* I tapped her shoulder. "I know who it is," I said.

She swiveled on her heels and shone the flashlight directly up onto my face. "Of course you do," she said.

I gestured helplessly. "I was sitting next to her at the dinner," I said.

I was getting her resigned look again. "Of course you were. So?"

She still had the phone to her ear. "Regina," I said, then realized. "Oh, my God, Julie. The woman who's onstage? The singer? It's her partner."

Julie muttered something that might and might not have been *fuck*. "Get over here," she said into the phone and clicked it off, standing up as she did. If I'd been squatting that long, I'd never have gotten up again. "Last name?"

I shook my head. "We didn't get that far. She went to medical school with Thea, though."

She made the connection immediately. "Thea Madison. She was the doctor got called out," she said, frowning.

We looked at each other for a long moment. "Listen," said Julie, and then suddenly Jordan was standing next to me and staring down at the high-tops. "No," she said.

"Jordan." I put my hand on her arm, holding her away from doing—what? "I'm so sorry."

"No!" She looked at Julie. "Reggie's all right, isn't she? She doesn't hold her liquor very well sometimes. She—" Julie's face, impassive, told the truth. "No," said Jordan again, but it was in despair. She turned toward me, blindly, and I put my arms around her and held her. "It's going to be all right," I said automatically, possibly the stupidest remark I've ever made. It was never going to be all right ever again, not for Jordan.

Julie said, more gently than I'd have thought possible, "I'm sorry for your loss. Ms.—?"

Jordan was sobbing. I said, helplessly, "I don't know."

"Okay." Julie raised her voice. "Everyone back in the dining-room, please." A couple of stubborn hold-outs appeared rooted to the spot; Julie wasn't having it. "That means you, too, okay? Now! And nobody leaves." The last bit was said in the direction of the hapless manager, who started wringing his hands again. "Of course," he said. "Of course." He turned and started herding women back in.

"And I need some light out here."

A second later he hit the floodlights, and suddenly everything was dazzling bright, gargoyles lurking behind bushes, shadows shifting dangerously. Somewhere out there was someone who had killed a woman.

Julie was still staring at me, her mind working fast. I think she was about to tell me to leave, too; I'm pretty sure she wanted to. But Jordan was continuing to cling, and short of physically transferring her over to Julie, I didn't know what I could do about it. Julie frowned and turned back to the body in the bushes, her flashlight beam probing. The wind shifted and a few dead leaves swirled on the pathway, and we could hear voices from the dining-room, Char arguing with the manager about something.

"Regina Sanborn," said Julie. She had Reggie's wallet in her hand. I noticed for the first time that she was wearing gloves. When had she put those on? Did she always bring all that gear with her to a dinner party? Flashlight, gloves, what else? "From Halifax." She glanced up. "She's Canadian."

"They both are," I said, over Jordan's head. She was still sobbing.

"Uh-huh." She went back to looking in the wallet. I had a sudden sense of déjà vu: this wasn't the first time I'd stood with Julie Agassi over a woman's body while she checked the ID. Maybe there was something wrong with me after all. Maybe I was a death-magnet. Something like that.

In the meantime, I was holding a sobbing woman and the shoulder of my dress was getting wet and I had no idea what to do about either. Miss Manners is strangely silent on the etiquette for situations such as this.

Come to think of it, there probably *aren't* any situations like this. Not even vaguely approximating it. Unless you happen to be me. If anyone gets killed in Provincetown, chances are I'm going to be involved in some way.

Miss Manners would be horrified.

I was saved by the arrival of Julie's reinforcements, official and bustling in their uniforms, stretching crime-scene tape and flashing photographs.

Julie touched Jordan on the shoulder. "I'm sorry," she said gently, "but we have to talk."

Still crying, Jordan freed me and nodded, wiping her hand under her nose, oblivious to everything around her. "Yes. Okay."

"Okay," Julie said, her voice encouraging. "Your name is?"

Another sniffle. "Jordan Bellefort. That's—that's my partner. Reggie."

Julie said, "Regina Sanborn?"

"Yes. Reggie."

"Okay," Julie said again, then caught sight of me. "You can go, Sydney," she said. "I have some questions for you, but later."

Jordan said, "I don't want to be alone—"

"Thea," I decided. "I'll go get Thea." Julie looked at me sharply. "Dr. Madison," I said.

"Fine," Julie said, and turned back to Jordan. "And you were performing tonight..."

I ducked under the crime-scene tape that was up against the doors and slipped inside, where it was—thankfully—a lot warmer. What with my dress wet in spots, I'd been feeling the wind.

The banquet room looked like the aftermath of a natural disaster. Women sat or stood around in clusters, pale and serious, talking together in low, shocked voices. I found Thea in the wide sweeping hallway, talking to the manager. She caught sight of me over his shoulder. "Is it true?"

I nodded. In my haste to help Jordan, I'd forgotten that Thea had a history with Reggie, too. Medical school. That conversation felt like it had taken place a lifetime before, not half an hour. "Thea, I'm so sorry."

She took a deep breath. "Where's Jordan?"

"Outside with Julie Agassi. I came to get you. I think Jordan could use some support."

"We both could," Thea said. "Hell, Sydney, what *happened*?"

"I have no idea," I said helplessly. "Julie said suspicious death, that's all. I don't know how—"

"I mean, I wasn't in the room," Thea said, intent on her own reasoning. "I had to go see to that guest."

"Char came to the mic and said someone needed a doctor," I said. Julie had clicked onto that right away; it was taking me longer. "You'd have been the one to go if you'd been in the room. You're the local doctor; Reggie's just visiting." I hesitated. "If this really is a murder—"

"—then it could have been me who was killed," said Thea. "Does someone want me dead?" Her voice was blank, flat.

"Or it's that someone wanted to make sure Reggie was the doctor to respond," I said. "What was up with the guest you attended to? Could they have been faking?"

She shrugged. "Maybe. I couldn't see any swelling. I put a bandage on it and told her to take some ibuprofen. The front desk people only called me because of potential liability."

"Did they see her fall?"

She shook her head. "I don't know. I didn't ask." She looked worried. "I'd better get out to see Jordan," she said.

"Thea. Be careful."

I watched her go, uneasy. What if Thea *had* been the intended victim, and the killer didn't know there would be another doctor at the dinner? What if they had another go at her once they realized she was still alive? But who would want to kill Thea? Who would want to kill *Reggie*?

Even if it were the case that the killer was still after Thea, the safest place she could be right now was with Julie. And maybe I was getting ahead of myself. Maybe this wasn't murder.

Yeah, Riley. Because natural causes usually end up putting a body in the shrubbery.

I wandered back into the banquet room. Char was talking to a group by the stage and I drifted over toward them. She caught sight of me and signaled to me to come over. "What's going on, Sydney?"

"I don't know, exactly," I hedged. Julie wouldn't thank me if I said too much. I looked around the circle of concerned faces. Nice women, caring women. Was one of them a killer? Had any of them followed Reggie out of the room when she went to tend to the person who'd cut themselves?

Who had cut themselves? That was where she needed to start. "Who asked you to call for a doctor?" I asked Char. Good place to start.

"The bartender," she said without hesitating. "I don't know his name. He said someone had cut themselves clearing dishes."

The banquet room was down a long, wide hallway from the kitchen, which also served the inn's small bar and restaurant. Servers brought food on trolleys to the buffet tables. People were always going in and out of that room: diners getting second or third helpings, servers replenishing depleted dishes. It was high-traffic and sometimes crowded. The bar was set up in the banquet room. "How did he know?" I asked.

"What?"

"How did he know someone got cut?"

"I don't know, Sydney," said Char, a little impatiently. "I'm just telling you what happened."

Julie must have called in everyone who worked for the department, whether on duty or not. They were letting people leave, but everyone had to stop at the door and speak to a couple of officers getting names and contact information, asking them questions. In the buffet room, another officer was talking to the staff.

The bartender was nowhere to be seen.

Julie came up to me, her eyes scanning the room. Cop's eyes; they notice everything, all the time, no matter where they are, no matter what they're doing. I knew; Ali did the same thing every time he walked into a room. It was second nature. "You learn anything?" she asked.

"About what?"

"Don't play games," she said, her gaze coming back to me with a click that was almost audible. "I know you, Sydney. You think you're the main character in some TV British crime show. You've been asking questions."

I said, neutrally, "The bartender told Char someone had cut themselves and needed a doctor. Char didn't see where he went after that, she was busy making the announcement, and then bringing Jordan up to the stage." I paused. "Um, the thing is, said bartender doesn't seem to be here anymore."

She looked over at the empty bar, a reflex action. "This was how long after they asked Dr. Madison to go to the lobby?"

I thought about it for a moment. "Two minutes, maybe. Three. Not much more than that. It was between Poppy's act and Zoe's."

She nodded. "Okay. Thanks, Sydney. You can go whenever you want."

I hesitated. "Are you calling in South Yarmouth?" In Massachusetts, homicides are investigated by the state police. Once it was clear what she was dealing with—and Julie surely was clear about what she was dealing with—she would have to turn the case over to the Staties. The operation never gave her any joy.

"Just gathering some preliminary information," she said pleasantly. "We'll get to that later if it's necessary."

I saw Thea and Jordan come back in; Thea had found a sweater somewhere and wrapped it around Jordan, who was visibly shaking.

"Excuse me," I said to Julie, and headed over to them. "Hey, hi. Is there anything I can do?"

Thea said, "Hey, Sydney. Yeah, you know, actually, there is. Jordan doesn't want to stay here tonight. The police have been in their room, and… well, anyway, can she go stay at the Race Point? Do you have a room she can use? I'd bring her to my house, only I have people staying there because of Women's Week." Thea lived in a big beautiful octagonal house in the West End. I was pretty sure her friends lined up to be able to stay there.

"Of course." I didn't know what we had available at the inn, but we always have one or two rooms we keep open for surprise VIPs— or emergencies. This definitely qualified, maybe as both. "Let's get your things and I'll drive you there." I had come to the inn in my somewhat disreputable elderly Honda Civic, known locally as the Little Green Car for the excellent reason that it was, in fact, a little green car. I've never been terribly good at naming mechanical contraptions. Nor have I ever questioned the assumption that I should.

Name them, that is.

Thea still had her arm around Jordan's shoulders. "Okay? Sydney will go to your room with you and pick up what you need for tonight. I'll come by and see you tomorrow. Is that good?"

Jordan looked hollow-eyed. She nodded. She hadn't said a word yet.

Thea fished in her purse for a moment and pulled out a small envelope. I had no idea what something that small could be used for; it looked like it could hold a couple of business cards. "Xanax," she said, handing it to me. "She's had one; give her one before she goes to bed. You'll stay with her, right?"

"I will?" I hadn't been planning to, but now that Thea said it, I couldn't imagine dropping Jordan off and abandoning her. "Yeah, of course." Ibsen was going to have to forgo his nightly thyroid-pill-and-treats routine.

"Good. I'll come by in the morning."

In the morning I'd have to get ready for another wedding. Life was going to go on. Always a shock to the bereaved, that nothing had changed, whereas, for them, everything had.

Jordan and Reggie's room was down at the end of one of the long wings; the walk seemed interminable. There was crime-scene tape over the door, but Julie must have left word, because the lone officer on guard let us in. "I have to write down everything you take," he said, apologetically, to Jordan.

She nodded and sat down on the bed, staring into nothingness, what she probably thought was the nothingness of her whole life stretching out emptily before her. I found a bag and asked her which clothes were hers, packed jeans and sneakers and a sweater, found a toothbrush and makeup kit in the bathroom, and called it a day. She didn't say anything else when we walked to the car and even once we were in it. "It's cold," I said, fiddling with the heater, which worked on a timer known only to itself. "I'll try and get some heat up for you here."

"Thank you." It was the first thing I'd heard Jordan say since I'd left her with Julie outside the banquet room. She seemed very small, curled into the passenger seat beside me. So different from her stage presence, which was gigantic. "Detective Agassi thinks someone killed Reggie," she said. "On purpose."

Being dumped in the bushes had kind of given that part away, but I didn't say it. I pulled out of the circle and drove up toward Bradford Street. Keeping my eyes on the road, I said carefully, "That's what it seems. Did you—do you know anybody who would wish her harm?" As in the ultimate harm.

I felt her shaking her head. "She was a *doctor*," she said, and there was no mistaking what was in her voice now: anguish. "She *helped* people. Who would want to kill someone who helps people?"

"I don't know." The words were automatic; the question had been rhetorical.

The Race Point Inn doesn't have a parking lot—parking's at a premium in Provincetown at any time, and on Commercial Street.... well, let's just say that last year I saw a private parking place for sale on Zillow. For one car. Not covered, no amenities. Eighty-five thousand dollars.

In some places, that's the mortgage on a condo. Not here.

But it was October, and so I was able to find a spot on the street not far from the inn. I hefted Jordan's bag over my shoulder and we set off. More to fill the air with conversation than anything else, I said, "I think you'll like the Race Point. We actually have more than one building here. The main part of it was a sea captain's house built in 1840, with a carriage house and a guest house and some other miscellaneous buildings part of the whole." It stretched all the way between Commercial and Bradford streets, with Adrienne the diva chef's restaurant along with two additional dining rooms and three bars, one of them outside by the pool, and even a patio and bower where I arranged weddings. It was huge. My first boss, Barry, bought it thirty-odd years ago and spent a full two years restoring it before he opened for business. He hired me one winter day when I was leaving a bad relationship and needed a new start. I had loved him, deeply and sincerely.

I'd been the one who found Barry's body floating in the pool one summer morning. I didn't think I should share that bit with Jordan.

Mike—the inn's manager—was at the front desk, doing something. He looked moderately pleased to see me, glancing up over the half-glasses he was wearing these days to read anything.

Mike and I have a history. On a once-upon-a-time chilly October night that was colder than this one, he had saved my life; I'd returned the favor last spring, somewhat spectacularly breaking my arm in the process. Four months on, I was still traveling to Orleans twice a week for physical therapy. "Hey, Sydney. How was the dinner?"

I was mildly surprised. Mike is always on Facebook and usually is the first to know when

anything happens in town; the fact that he
didn't know about Reggie yet either said
there'd been a crisis here he'd had to attend to,
or his mad social media skills were slipping.
"Not so good," I said. "Listen, Mike, I need a
room. This is Jordan." I couldn't remember
her last name. "Jordan was staying at the Provincetown Inn, but—well, there was an accident tonight, and her partner—"

Jordan said, "is dead."

Mike read my expression; we know each
other pretty well. "No problem," he said easily.
"I have a suite."

"Can we do the check-in tomorrow?" I
asked. "Jordan needs to get some rest."

"Of course." He fiddled with the key card
machine and handed me two cards. "Atwood,"
he told me. The rooms at the Race Point Inn
are named for streets in Provincetown.

"Thanks, Mike. I'm staying, too."

He nodded. "Okay."

The suite made it easier. I got Jordan in
and installed her in the bedroom with her bag
beside her; there was just so much nursemaid-
ing I wanted to do. Filled a glass with water,
gave her Thea's Xanax, watched her swallow
it. "I'll be in the next room," I said, and she

nodded. I left her sitting on the edge of the bed, staring into space.

I called Mike from my mobile. "Can you get someone to cover the desk so we can talk?" I'd actually been a little surprised he'd been there; he usually had a phalanx of young sexy guys to staff reception. And clean the pool. And…

"Of course; Jacques is on tonight anyway. I was just covering his break when you came in. Are you all right?"

"If you'll bring me a glass of wine," I said, "I'll tell you all about it.

4

By the next morning, everyone in Provincetown knew what had happened.

You can't keep secrets in a small town, and especially not when so many people are present when something happens that you might have wanted to keep secret. Before they even left the banquet hall, women were pulling out their mobile phones, taking photographs, posting to Twitter and Facebook and Instagram.

Ali had seen it, and called me a little after seven. "Are you all right?"

"Yeah." I'd just spent an uncomfortable night on the sofa in Jordan's suite. The Xanax had worked like a charm for her; I, on the other hand, had spent a whole lot of time staring at the ceiling, sleep elusive. My arm was aching, and I spent a good bit of the night wondering if it would ever get back to normal.

It didn't hurt all the time, but when it did, it was pretty intense. Like when I was trying to sleep on someone's sofa.

"What happened?"

I sighed and tried to stretch out a crick in my neck. "A woman got killed at the dinner," I said. "I don't know how, and I barely met her before she was killed, but I'm sort of involved…" Some people seem to think I attract murder and murderous thoughts, but I really didn't see how my supposedly dark karma had reached over to the seat next to me and grabbed Reggie.

"Sydney—" Ali worries about me. Being in law enforcement, he has a different worldview than most of the rest of us. He expects the worst.

Sometimes he's right.

"It didn't have anything to do with me," I said. "I mean, not really. Except that we were sitting at the same table. That's really all. And afterward, when the police let us leave—well, I brought her partner back to the Race Point with me, because she didn't want to stay in her old room at the Provincetown Inn and anyway she couldn't, there was crime-scene tape. That's all." That, and the very cold feeling I had all over. One moment we'd been sitting and talking and I'd even admired those absurd rainbow high-tops; the next she was dead. "It was after the actual dinner, people were still having dessert, they'd started the entertainment." I was babbling, I knew; I'd already babbled, last night, to Mike, who instead of a glass of wine had brought me a bottle and had listened gravely as I talked my way through it, talking way too much and for far too long.

Apparently I hadn't babbled enough of it out yet. "She was—she was nice, Ali. She was Canadian."

He wanted for me to continue, and when I didn't, he observed mildly, "Well, they have that reputation. For being nice, you know."

I blew out a long exhalation. "It all started out so—"

"—innocently?" he supplied.

"—interestingly," I corrected. "It was the first time they'd ever been to the States. Jordan—that's the dead woman's partner, who's here at the inn—she performs all over Canada, she's a singer, and Reggie—she's the one who got killed—was a physician in Halifax. She went to medical school with Thea." I don't know why that detail seemed relevant. "Jordan was singing at the dinner, but she's also here doing family research. Genealogy." That conversation seemed to have taken place in a different era, on a different plane of existence.

He wasn't about to be diverted. "Sydney? Are you really all right?"

I took a deep breath, exhaled. "Yeah. No, really, I am. I have to be. I still have weddings this week, and Jordan's going to need a lot of support to get through all this, too."

"You know," Ali observed, "you don't *have* to be the one to help her through it."

"I know," I said.

But we both knew I didn't really believe it.

I left Jordan a note—it looked like she was going to still be under for a while—and headed back to my apartment on Carver Street. The town was still, and fog had moved in off the water, moisture sticking cold and clammy to my face and neck. It didn't bother me: I love Provincetown in the early mornings, when no one else is around and you can imagine what it was like back in the day, when the whaling ships docked at the piers and the town supported occupations like ship's chandlers and coopers. Or even after that, when nearly everyone made their living from the fish that gave Cape Cod its name. Now yachts and ferries, whale-watches and sports-fishing excursion boats tie up there, and their cargo is people.

There's still a commercial fishing fleet here, but it's dwindled to a handful of boats, and you have to wonder how much longer they'll survive.

Ibsen let me know in no uncertain terms how little he'd appreciated my absence. I gave him some treats, scratched him somewhat absent-mindedly, stripped off my clothes, and stepped into the shower.

I do some of my best thinking in the shower.

Jordan was right: it was hard to believe someone specifically wanted Reggie dead. This was her first time in Provincetown; hell, she lived in another *country*, for heaven's sake, this was her first time in the United States. Surely if someone there had wanted her dead, she'd have been killed in Nova Scotia? And no one *here* could have wanted her dead; no one here even *knew* her.

So theoretically she shouldn't be dead at all.

Was it a case of mistaken identity? I'd dealt with such a situation once before, during a different October, a different sort of festival.

Anyway, who else could a killer be targeting? Jordan? Same objections apply. Thea? She's tiny and not easily confused with anyone else, if for no other reason than she wears more beads in her hair—simultaneously—than craft-supply stores carry on their shelves. I closed my eyes and put my face under the spray. Had my friend Eileen been at the dinner? Margie from Eastham? I couldn't remember. There had been a lot of women there I didn't know, of course, and an intended victim could have been one of them.

But if that were the case, she hadn't collected her murderer here. We who make our livings from tourism occasionally daydream they'll all die—especially when Augustitis hits—but we don't go so far as to actually kill any of them. At least not yet. If the intended victim were one of the visitors, then she'd brought the killer with her in some way. So why Provincetown? Why not do it wherever she lived?

I turned off the water and stepped out of the shower, wrapping a towel around myself. No: it had to be Reggie. Someone had known she was a doctor. Someone had lured Thea away so it would be Reggie who answered the call.

Why?

***

I got back to the inn in time to escort the florist who'd just arrived out to the patio where we do weddings; it's behind a locked iron grille for privacy. It's a pretty space we offer, though I do say so myself: over just beyond the pool, it's a pretty, shaded space with a bower, flexible seating, and cool stone flags underfoot. The florist was from out of town, and clearly didn't know our setup. She looked at the bower a little grimly. "I should have brought someone to help."

Years ago I would have heard the hint and felt obligated to step in and give her a hand, but I'd learned a few things over time. "Feel free to call someone," I said cheerfully. "Let me know if you need anything else."

I headed over to Mike's office first. He looked up from a ledger. "How's your head?"

"Fine," I said, puzzled. "Why?"

He raised his eyebrows. "An empty bottle of Châteauneuf-du-Pape wants to know," he said.

"What kind of lightweight do you take me for?" We both knew it was bravado: we'd each seen the other drunk before. And dealt with the consequences. "Has Jordan come down yet?"

"She's in the dining room," he said. "Julie Agassi called. She wants Jordan to stay put."

"Julie's bringing in the state police," I concluded, nodding. She had to. "Bet she wants to talk to Jordan alone first." It was always a sore spot, handing murders over to them. If she could change anything about the way the Commonwealth did things, I suspected that's what she'd choose. Julie was a good detective. Even a good homicide detective.

Not that Provincetown has that many murders. Normally our crime waves involve bicycle theft, and that only during the summer tourist season, when everyone who arrives in a car ditches it as soon as they come to the conclusion that bicycles are the only really viable means of transportation in an overcrowded town.

Still, the murders we do have? Julie would prefer to be the one who solved them. And to be fair, she generally does figure them out first.

Occasionally I get to help.

"Well, she's not here yet," said Mike. "In case you wanted to know."

I grinned; I couldn't help it. "I love you, you know."

"As well you should," he said, returning to his ledger.

Jordan was drinking coffee and ignoring a plate filled with fabulous treats wrought by Angus, our pastry chef. I paused by her table. "Jordan? Good morning. Do you mind if I join you?"

She looked at me, lassitude in her eyes. I'd seen that before. Last spring, during the film festival, an award recipient got bashed over the head with the award itself; I'd seen that same look in the eyes of his newly married—and newly widowed—husband.

Jordan reached over and pulled a chair out slightly from the table. I took it as an invitation and sat down. "How are you feeling?"

"I'm all right," she said, picking up her coffee cup and then setting it down again as she realized it was empty. I looked around and gestured to the server. "You know," Jordan was saying, "the thing is, I really am all right. I feel like I should be–I don't know, crying, screaming, something, eh? But I'm all right."

Shock, I thought. "Everybody is different," I told her. The server—was it Jeff? Jay? Jack?—came over to refill her cup and put one in front of me. "Can I get you anything else?" he asked. Jordan shook her head. I made as discreet a shooing motion as I could, and he left.

Jordan stared into the cup. "We hadn't really had a holiday in a long time," she said. "Reggie has her practice at the clinic, and I was traveling so much for work I just wanted to stay home with her when I had time off. There was always something to be done at home and I was always falling behind. Errands, you know? Chores? And we both have volunteer stuff we do. If I hadn't been doing this research, I wouldn't have gotten my manager to sign me on to perform, and we wouldn't have come." She raised her eyes to my face. "Is this my fault? Did she get killed because of me? Because I brought her here? My obsession with my ancestry?"

"No," I said firmly. That at least I knew; that at least I had learned. "This is one person's fault. It's the fault of the person who did it. That's all. They're the one to blame. Not you."

She nodded but I could tell she was humoring me. "All right," she said, unconvinced, and drank some coffee.

I finally tasted mine; the inn makes really excellent coffee. Angus' own special blend; Adrienne the diva chef wouldn't stoop to select beverages. In her world, there were sommeliers for that.

"Listen," I said to Jordan. "Detective Agassi? Julie? You met her last night. She's coming over here soon to ask you some questions, and after that there'll be some men from the state police." I was fairly safe in that prediction: in all the times the Staties had invaded our town to detect something, they'd always been male. "But Julie—well, she's closer to us. She's taking Reggie's death very much to heart. So— I'm just saying—help her if you can." What I was doing was probably illegal. I took a deep breath. "It's okay if she figures it out and they get the credit."

"I don't care who gets the credit," Jordan said. She looked around the room, her eyes unfocused, unseeing. "I just want her back."

I just want her back. The cry of all the bereaved. Don't let this be real. Let me rewind, go back to that moment, the split-second before the only moment that mattered, let me do something different, change the outcome. Some people think it wouldn't matter, that fate won't be denied, that the universe would just work it out to get to the same result via a different route. Once fate has you in its sights, it's all over.

The bereaved? They all believe they could change it. If they were just given the chance.

I put my hand, tentatively, on Jordan's arm. "I know," I said. What else can you say? I thought for a moment. "Jordan, was anything happening back home, anything that seemed wrong or out of place?" Starting with broad strokes might be the way to go. We could nail down specifics later. Maybe she knew, already, that something had followed them here, the monster that had been shadowing Reggie.

She shook her head. "No," she said. "You don't understand. Everyone loved Reggie." I started to say something and she half-turned toward me, focused now, intent. "Listen to me. I know they say everyone has enemies. But Reggie volunteered at a the Africville heritage site. She worked in a neighborhood clinic. She sang in the choir at our church. She was completely apolitical, she never got into arguments, if anything ever heated up she walked away. There's nothing there for anyone to dislike."

I moistened my lips and asked the question. "What about you?"

"What about me? What do you mean?"

I withdrew my hand and wrapped it around my coffee cup. She had to do this one alone. "Is there anything about you, about your life, that would make anyone want *you* dead?"

"You mean you think they killed Reggie because they thought it was me? You're saying they couldn't tell the difference between one Black woman and another?" Anger in her voice, now.

"That's not what I meant." But it was, in a way. "Maybe it's you they wanted, but it was easier to get to her." I said, gently, "I'm just asking, Jordan. The police will want to know, too. It's happened before."

"It happens all the time," she said bleakly.

But she wasn't talking about Reggie anymore.

5

Mirela called midmorning. "I am going to Beech Forest, sunshine," she said. Beech Forest is out in the National Seashore, a pond with a hiking trail around it, ducks and geese, picnic tables. A birdwatcher's paradise. Beyond it, the dunes, the beaches, the Atlantic Ocean.

"Congratulations," I said. I was feeling a little snippy; I hadn't handled things well with Jordan, and I was feeling unsettled; I could have, *should* have done better. Julie had arrived, promptly gave me The Look, and for once I had the sense to get out of there.

"Congratulations to you, too, because you are driving us there," said Mirela.

"How do you know I'm not busy?"

"Because you told me of your weddings this week," she replied. "And you do not have one until four o'clock today."

I scowled at my calendar. It was mounted on the wall over my desk in the cubbyhole behind Reception that passes for my office. I didn't remember giving Mirela the schedule, but I probably had. I often do things I don't later remember, especially if there's alcohol involved. "I don't feel like going," I said. Even to my own ears I sounded petulant. "Take your own car. Take a taxi."

"Sunshine, you are in a mood," Mirela informed me. "The air will do you good. Come and pick us up in half an hour. And bring some applesauce, sunshine, otherwise you will have to take me to the market, too."

Applesauce, God help us. I checked my watch: 10:30. Not a good time to be venturing into the kitchen; it was the edge of the liminal divide between Angus being in charge and the arrival of Adrienne the diva chef. I most emphatically did not want to ask Adrienne the diva chef for applesauce. The Stop & Shop would be a lot easier.

Walking to Boston on cut glass to get it would be a lot easier.

But I also didn't want to be a bad sport, and I was, after all, trying to fit Lily's existence into my worldview, so I headed cautiously out to the cavernous kitchens at the back of the inn, the domain of Adrienne the diva chef and her minions. Fortunately for me, it was one of the minions in residence: Philip the sous-chef, busily grinding something in a food processor. Behind him, a five-tiered wedding cake that was about the same size as my Little Green Car.

I waited until the machine was finished. "Holy moly, that's for the four o'clock?"

"Hey, doll," he said, offering me his lips for a quick kiss. "And yes, indeed it is, and you should be glad, girl, that you weren't here two hours ago when Angus was swearing a blue streak at it."

I hopped up on the counter across from him, something I wouldn't have dared do had either Angus or Adrienne the diva chef been in the vicinity. "Why are all chefs so temperamental?" I asked.

"We're *artistes*, that's why, doll. Now just let me pop my panko breadcrumbs in the oven—there we go—and I'm all yours. Woo-whee, that's hot! And speaking of hot, what brings *you* down into the bowels of hell?"

"I'm in search of applesauce," I said.

"What kind?"

"There are different kinds?"

"Well, Adrienne has a recipe she says—"

I held up my hand. "Just applesauce," I said firmly. "The kind you get at the supermarket in little plastic tubs."

He gave a moue of disgust. "Never talk about supermarket products in here," he cautioned. "I'm surprised you let those *words* cross your lips, much less any of the applesauce in question."

"It isn't for me," I said. "It's for Mirela's little girl. She's apparently just started real food."

"Doll," said Philip, shaking his head, "applesauce in plastic tubs is not, but *not*, real food. Forcing someone to eat it is probably against the Geneva Convention. Besides, not that I would know, of course, but I hear there's an entire aisle at the supermarket containing what is euphemistically called baby food." He shuddered. "I don't think one could in all honesty refer to that as real food, either."

"I don't think Mirela cares much about what's proper baby food. She has her own ideas about what's right for Lily."

"Well, let me see what we have. I know Angus occasionally puts some in a couple of his recipes." He disappeared back into the shadows of the big kitchen and I looked around for something to eat. It was bleak.

Something I'll never understand: when they're not being used, industrial kitchens never look like there's any food there. Ever. There used to be a documentary series called *Life After People*, showing how cities and jungles and the oceans would change if humanity suddenly disappeared from the face of the earth. Industrial kitchens, when they're not in use, look a whole lot like Day One of *Life After People*. "Isn't there anything to eat around here?"

"What was that, doll?" Philip reappeared with a jar in his hand. "Here you go."

"Where do all Angus' leftover pastries go?"

"*Angus'* leftovers? *Please*, Sydney! What is that supposed to mean?" He looked at me and gave an exaggerated sigh. "All right, then, I'll get you something if you'll give me the dish on this murder."

"How would I know anything about that?"

"Uh-huh. You don't know anything about murder like I don't know anything about evening gowns." When he wasn't working, Philip performed in a drag act at the Crown & Anchor. "They're our *hobbies*, doll."

He disappeared again and returned with a chocolate croissant. "Be grateful. I was saving

67

it for my own lovely self. Now tell Auntie Philip *everything*."

I took a bite of flaky buttery pastry first. Heaven. I'd been tempted by the plate at Jordan's breakfast table, but it would have been crass to have helped myself, so I exercised considerable restraint and hadn't. "One of the women at the dinner was killed," I said. "Right when her partner was onstage, performing. She's a singer. The partner, that is. The woman who got killed is a doctor."

"And? Well?"

"And nothing. They're Canadian. The woman who was killed? You know my friend Thea? Dr. Madison at Outer Cape Health? They went to medical school together." I swallowed. "She was wearing this perfect pair of rainbow sneakers…"

He shuddered again, though whether it was at the murder or the sartorial choice I couldn't tell. "And who did it?"

"I don't know." I took another bite of croissant, chewed, swallowed. "I don't even know *how* they did it."

"Doll, you're disappointing me gravely." He reached over and grabbed the remainder of the croissant, tore it, and popped half into his mouth.

"Hey!"

"So there. Bring me more information, you'll earn more chocolate."

I made a face at him and hopped down off the counter. "Thanks for the applesauce."

"Anytime, doll. Kiss-kiss." He was busy finishing off the pastry.

I left the inn and hiked up High Pole Hill to the parking space I rent at the Pilgrim Monument lot. The monument is a tower curiously modeled after one in Italy (no one seems to know why), built to commemorate Provincetown as the Pilgrim's first landfall; the Mayflower Compact was written in our harbor. They didn't find any fresh water and ended up settling in Plymouth instead, but we like feeling smug about having been first.

As I did every time I climbed the hill, I reminded myself that I really should consider a gym membership. At this rate I was going to qualify for the one at the Council on Aging before I did anything about it.

I was also thinking. How *had* Reggie been killed? I hadn't seen blood. It had to have been quick, and quiet, which did argue for a knife… but that was a bad idea, too: I'm no forensics expert, but even I know that arterial blood spray is significant. And the murderer had to walk through the inn to get from the banquet room to the front lobby; no one was going to do that covered in blood.

Which left what? Strangulation? Asphyxia? (Were they the same thing?) If this were a spy movie, maybe a broken neck; spies in the thrillers Ali reads seem to know a quick trick, a twist, that does the job in seconds. Come to think of it, Ali himself could probably perform the maneuver. Eww. Best not to think about that.

The real question, though, was: would Julie tell me?

The Little Green Car started on the first try, which is always reassuring, and Mirela and Lily were waiting on the sidewalk when I pulled up in front of their condo. Lily looked like she was bundled for a trip to the Arctic; Mirela just looked beautiful. Mirela always looks beautiful. She has that fine, wheat-colored blonde hair and striking eyes that are almost violet and she looks better when she first gets out of bed in the morning than I do after an hour in front of the makeup mirror.

Right. Like I have a makeup mirror.

At Beech Forest, Mirela unpacked Lily's stroller and we made the obligatory circuit of the pond (with its two hills, and that mythical gym membership was prodding me all the way) before settling in to one of the picnic tables. I'd brought the applesauce; Mirela had brought a Thermos of Bloody Mary's for us and a packet of stale bread for the geese. "You're not supposed to feed them," I pointed out. "If a ranger comes by, you're in trouble."

"Sometimes, sunshine," said Mirela, "you must take a risk."

I poured some of the cocktail concoction into one of the mugs she'd pulled from her backpack and took a tentative sip. "Tell me," I said carefully, "if you wanted to kill someone with a hundred people in the next room, how would you do it?"

She pulled out a plastic bag with accoutrements—lemon wedges, celery sticks, and olives—and handed it to me. "I would be quick, and I would be quiet," she said.

"Yeah, I got that. But how?"

She shrugged and poured her drink. "A knife," she said. "Poison would be better, but it is not fast enough."

"Not even close," I agreed. "But a knife leaves you covered in blood."

She frowned, thinking. "Is it a man or a woman who has done this thing?"

"Probably a man," I said. "The bartender disappeared right around that time. I'm sure they're looking for him."

"Then it will be strangling," she decided. "It is easy if you use wire."

I didn't ask how she knew it would be easy. A cloud drifted in front of the sun, and Lily started fussing; it was as if the day itself were turning dark, ominous. I half-remembered that some culture was superstitious about talking about death.

Oh, yeah, that's right: Americans.

"Sunshine," Mirela said, "you know we cannot decide like this. If you want to know more, you have to learn more."

"That sounded clever," I said, sipping my drink. I was enjoying it a little too much. My inn does a fabulous and famous brunch, with Bloody Mary's a specialité de la maison, but I never went. How did people drink alcohol before noon and still manage to get through the day?

Lily was making some kind of gurgling noise. "Is she all right?"

Mirela picked the baby up in a move that looked practiced; she made it look easy. Mirela makes everything look easy. "She wants her applesauce," she translated.

"How could you tell?"

She gave me a look, balanced Lily delicately on her lap, and unscrewed the top to the applesauce jar, taking a taste of it herself first. "It is good."

"Of course it's good. I had to brave Adrienne the diva chef for that." I paused. "The problem is, I don't see my next move here. I don't see how to get more information. Julie Agassi's not going to tell me anything, and the Staties are in town."

Without looking up from what she was doing, Mirela said, "Then you will ask this woman's partner."

"Jordan?"

"She is at your inn, no? Then go and ask her. You can be her friend. If I were in her place, I would want for a friend right now."

"And if she doesn't?"

She leveled me a look. "Be persuasive."

***

Billy, Jordan's manager, had moved the rest of Jordan's—and, as it turned out, Reggie's—things into her suite at the Race Point. She was back up there, having apparently already been through the preliminary tender mercies of the state police. I probably should have stayed with her; I hadn't yet met any of them who had anything close to a gentle and deft touch. "Sorry, Jordan."

She shrugged. "It's fine. Your friend Julie was here. And Billy, too." She smiled for the thin young white man sipping room-service coffee. He looked emaciated, but in a hip rather than unhealthy way. At least ten piercings that I could see.

"I'm sorry," I said to him, extending my hand. "We haven't met. I'm Sydney."

He shook it. "Billy," he said. He had a fringe of bleached-blonde hair almost over his eyes. He set his cup down and turned to Jordan. "I should go."

"Not on my account," I said quickly. If she was finding solace in the presence of someone familiar, I was all for that.

"It's okay," he said. "Have a meeting at the Crown & Anchor." I must have looked askance, because he added, "We have to cancel the rest of Jordan's appearances for the week, eh? They'll understand, but there's paperwork."

Of course. I hadn't even thought of that. "I'm sorry," I said, the only words that came

to mind. "People are—are people being understanding?"

He nodded. "Yeah. Like I said, it's just the
paperwork. No one expects her to…"

"Sing," said Jordan. Her voice was a little
faint, and I wished I knew her well enough that
I could go put my arm around her. "The only
thing that helps me."

"Not tonight," Billy said to her. "Once
you're back home, we'll see what we need to
reschedule." He paused, apparently struggling
for words. Billy didn't strike me as a guy who
was really good at expressing feelings. "You
just have to take care of yourself, Jordan."

She smiled at him, then turned to me. "I
don't know what I'd do without Billy," she
said.

"You'd make a lot less money," he said
with a smile. "Nice to meet you, Sydney."

"You, too," I said, and waited until the
door had closed behind him. "It's good you
have someone here you know," I said. Thea
had, after all, been Reggie's close friend, not
Jordan's.

"Yes," she said. "I'm lucky, aren't I?"

The words hung in the air between us,
bleak, unanswerable. I cleared my throat.
"How did it go with the state police?"

75

She shrugged. "They started out sounding like they thought I had something to do with it."

Yeah; that sounded about right. "I'm sorry," I said again. I sat down on the edge of one of the armchairs.

"It didn't matter." She still sounded exhausted. "It was obvious it couldn't have been me. A hundred women saw me performing."

Including Julie; she would have made short work of their questioning. "What are your plans?" I asked.

"I have to stay here for a while," she said. "At least a few days. I'd planned on staying longer. Maybe. I don't know." She sounded confused. "They'll be back later this afternoon to talk to me again, they said. They said—but, wait, is that all right?" She looked suddenly worried. "This room—"

I held up a hand. "It's fine, it's all good, you're welcome as long as you need it," I said. I'd square it with Mike and Glenn later.

She nodded, as if confirming something. "Thanks. There's a lot of—red tape—about taking..." She stopped, struggling. "About Reggie going home."

I could just imagine. "I'm sorry," I said again, uselessly.

"If I only had something to do," she said, almost angrily. "Thea said she'd stop by, but I can't just sit here and do nothing, watch Netflix like I'm on holiday." She seemed to catch herself, and sighed. "That's what we were supposed to be, eh?" she said. "On holiday—you call it vacation, I think. We were going to come stay here next week. Here, at your inn."

I wasn't sure what to make of that. I checked my watch. "Listen, I have to go set up for a wedding," I said. "Would you—well, I could use a hand, to tell the truth, if you're really not doing anything else." It would give her something to do, some sort of focus. I mentally reviewed the wedding in question. Flowers were already in place. The couple wasn't using one of the town officiants, which always irked me a little—we try and keep our cottage wedding industry robust here—opting instead to have a friend get her minister-for-a-day certificate and marry them. Twelve guests, four people in the wedding party. Music via iPhone and portable speaker. Another friend taking care of the photography.

It's not that I think people shouldn't be allowed to have their day their way; of course they should. Straight people have been coming to Provincetown forever to get married, for the same reason the artists all came—for the light. There's something unique, it would seem, about Provincetown's light. Mirela understands it; I don't, I'm not a visual artists, though I'm the first to admit it can be both pretty and dramatic, sometimes both at once. And then of course since 2004, when Massachusetts led the way in making marriage equality the law, P'town has become Wedding Destination Central, since from about the 1940s on we've had a substantial gay population, especially in the summer.

The result is people like me, people who make our livings out of other people's joy and commitment. And the thing is, we're really good at it. For us, it's a calling, probably precisely because for so very long marriage equality was nothing but a dream. I remember the first year I was in Provincetown, a male couple came to stay at the inn and wanted a simple wedding ceremony. They had been together for sixty-three years. Both of them well into their eighties, one using a walker to perambulate, and they were finally making this public declaration of their love.

That's the only wedding I've ever cried at.

And Provincetown loves a wedding! There's a pedicab company—it used to be owned by my friend Bruce, but a group of Bulgarian kids bought him out a few years ago, they're fearless—and often wedding parties will hire them to drive the couple down Commercial Street with a "just married" sign tacked to the back. The cheering they get is nearly deafening. It's not my experience—I'm not gay—but I think I can understand the ache of all those years of being told you're not as good as everybody else. That you're not deserving of the same rights.

Anyway, all that meant that weddings are important to us here, and we want to get them right. Most of the officiants I know, and certainly all the ones I call on, take what they're doing very much to heart. There's no one-size-fits-all in terms of ceremonies. They find out about the couple, craft something that works for them within the requirements of the Commonwealth of Massachusetts, find the perfect readings. And while bringing a friend to officiate means that the friend will indeed know you better than someone who hasn't been on your journey with you, it also in some ways negates the importance of being steeped in this place, this tradition, this experience. So yes; I'm always a little irked.

Still, there was a lot to get done: chairs to be arranged and champagne to put out, and that should keep Jordan nicely busy. I couldn't imagine sitting alone in that suite for hours. It was a very nice suite, mind you—everything at the Race Point is well-designed and well-thought-out—but there are times when you just don't want to be alone.

Or can't face the ghosts that come out when you are.

"I'll be ready in a minute," said Jordan.

It was too soon for Reggie to be a ghost, I decided. And if she were anywhere, she'd still be out at the Provincetown Inn, moving along its trimmed hedges and floral pathways, looking for Jordan. Looking for justice.

I shook the thought off. We have our own resident ghosts at the Race Point Inn, and while I wasn't altogether sure what I actually believed about them, I'd experienced ghosts for sure, and didn't particularly like thinking about it.

What did that say about the heaven that both Ali's and my religions believed existed, if hanging around here was preferable?

"I'm ready." She'd changed from the tracksuit she'd been wearing to breakfast (comfort clothing, I diagnosed, and who wouldn't want comfort clothing after what she'd been through?) into a neat pair of jeans and a long, flowing sweater of a color I believe is called burnt umber, with a matching scarf holding her hair at bay. Makeup that took a long time to look that natural. "Sydney?"

"Sorry." I'd been staring.

She gave a smile, perhaps her first all day. "You looked miles away."

I stood up. "I was thinking about ghosts," I said, without actually thinking about what I was saying, and regretted it immediately—*nice one, Riley*—but she didn't seem affronted. "Is there a ghost here? At the inn?"

Some people want to talk about their loss right away. Others want to hold it at bay until the dam breaks and they can't push the pain away any longer. "We have a couple of them, actually," I said, opening the door and ushering her out into the hallway.

"Tell me," she said. She was almost breathless. Anything to not think about Reggie? Okay; ghost stories were just as good as wedding prep to keep the mind occupied. "Well, this building started out as a captain's house, you know, back when Provincetown was the whaling capital of Massachusetts. There were over fifty piers and wharves back then, with all the sub-industries the whaling industry depended on, windmills to run the salt works, coopers and sail riggers and all that. It was the usual—a lot of very rich people owned and captained the boats, and a lot more people struggled working for them.

"What years are we talking?" asked Jordan.

She really *was* interested; in my experience with tourists, no one *ever* asks for dates.

"The native tribes and the early colonists did shore whaling," I said. "That was the nautical equivalent of low-hanging fruit, I suppose. But the industry really got going around the mid-1800s—maybe the 1820s, and then out to the end of the century? There was a decent fishing industry growing up alongside the whaling, but the Portland Gale destroyed a lot of the wharves and put an end to the whaling for good, and the fishing went downhill after that, too." I suddenly remembered the connection and stopped. "Wait—when was your ancestor here?"

"1851," said Jordan.

"So that makes sense," I said. "The whalers weren't in and out of the harbor that much, you understand: they went out for months and months, out to the south Atlantic off the African coast, even to the Pacific Ocean. But the fishermen were closer to home. Some went out for a week, maybe two; some just out for a day. Someone could have easily slipped out of the harbor at night and headed up the coast."

We started down the stairs. I was trying to remember the dates of the Civil War. Sometime around then, wasn't it?

Jordan said, "Tell me more about the inn. You said it was owned by a ship's captain. Do you know his name? Is he the ghost that haunts it now?"

"Give me a second," I said. I went over to the reception desk. One of Mike's myriad handsome young men was there; he had a never-ending supply of them, though off-season was more difficult, as they all seemed to go to Key West or Palm Springs to staff receptions desks there during their seasons. "Hi, can you get someone to bring the champagne out to the patio for me?"

He nodded. "Nothing much going on now, I can do it," he said easily. "Philip knows what you need?"

I nodded. "Martin's probably around, too," I said. "He can show you which part of the cellar it's in. Thanks a lot." Martin was the maître d', who managed the restaurant with a calm, cool manner that contrasted sharply with that of Adrienne the diva chef. He spent a fair amount of time boasting that he could handle her, like she was a wild animal he alone knew how to tame. Personally, I avoided her.

"No problem," said the kid cheerfully, and I went back to Jordan. "Come on, let's get the chairs set up," I said, and we went through out to the pool and the patio beyond it where the bower stood waiting, elegant and colorful.

It was another gorgeous day. October can be iffy on Cape Cod; we've even had nor'easters come in during Women's Week, and rain seems almost inevitable at some point. But this year was cooperating madly: the trees were stunning with brilliant colors, the air was sharp without being cold, and the sun was glorious.

"Just the usual wedding arrangement," I told her now. "Chairs on either side, an aisle in between." We started moving the stacks, and I got back to the story. "So, his name was William Dutton," I said. "The ship captain. He built the house—that's the older part of the inn, now—in 1835."

"Is William Dutton your ghost?"

I shook my head. "We don't think so. We have two, actually. One stays in the original part of the house, but from what everyone who sees it has to say, it's a woman. Maybe his wife, waiting for him to come home—he was lost at sea, his whole schooner sank on a trip, somewhere near New Caledonia. Long way from home. I can't imagine how long she waited until she realized he wasn't coming back."

"And all the other women," added Jordan. "The crew's families."

She was right: they, too, would wait. In tiny apartments and boarding houses, in the lanes and streets that made up the fishing village, in shacks out in the dunes, they waited. I wondered what it felt like, when the hope died. "Them, too," I said.

"What about the other ghost?" asked Jordan.

"We don't know who he is, really," I said. "He's more recent—well, I'm assuming that, since he's in the wing that wasn't added on until 1915. Maybe one of the artists, the bohemians who came in during World War One."

She dropped a chair. "Sorry. Clumsy. I don't know much about that time."

"The intelligentsia of Greenwich Village," I said. "They generally summered in France, but with the war on, they couldn't go. And life here then was cheaper—it was just a fishing village, you know? So they all came here, and then the artists fell in love with the light, and they stayed even after the war was over. The summer of 1916 was famous, the real beginning of P'town as an art colony." Heady days, those were, with Eugene O'Neill over in a dune shack and Edna St. Vincent Millay writing poetry in an attic and John Dos Passos pouring his soul out about America, bleeding all over the paper in anguish. I love that Provincetown mourns the death of poets and playwrights the way other places mourn movie stars and rock musicians.

Mirela could recite the names of all the artists who'd lived and worked here. I love that I know artists. Some people live their whole lives without ever meeting a true artist. In Provincetown, you can meet them all, and break bread with them and let them teach you how to look at the world.

I suddenly realized that Jordan had sat down on one of the chairs and was staring at me. "What? What is it? Are you okay?"

She said, "I haven't been completely honest with you, Sydney."

I sat down across the aisle from her. "That sounds serious," I said. "What is it?"

"We were staying at the Provincetown Inn because that's where they put the performers up," she said. "People like me, from out of town. But I was going to come here anyway. To your inn, I mean." She took a deep breath. "Here's the thing, Sydney, I'm pretty sure this, the Race Point Inn, or whatever the building was used for before, it was one of the stops on the Underground Railroad. And I think Sarah and Callie stayed here."

I'd never heard anything of the sort, and I'm pretty good with P'town history. Well, except the dates of the Civil War; fair point. "Why do you think so?"

"Callie's letters. My great-great-grand-mother. I told you, she could read and write. She kept journals, letters, everything."

"And she mentioned William Dutton?"

She shook her head. "No, no, not the name. And she didn't talk about an inn, either. Do you know when the house became an inn?" She shook her head before I could answer. "It doesn't matter. But anyway, I've been in touch with the historical commission, we've emailed back and forth, and apparently this is one of the buildings in town used by the Railroad. And since Callie's sister Sarah didn't make it to Halifax—well, maybe this is too fanciful, but I have to wonder if she's the one haunting you now. Callie did talk about Provincetown for sure, and it was positive, she was so pleased to be here—maybe Sarah felt the same way and just stayed on. Once she'd died, I mean. She died at sea, but she could have come back here, right? It's possible, isn't it?"

I had absolutely no idea how to respond. I didn't know what the rules were for hauntings. I wasn't even sure I believed in ghosts, except that I'd had experiences I couldn't explain. Not here in P'town... another place, another ghost.

I realized I was staring at Jordan. And that was something else. If it was common knowledge that we'd been part of the Underground Railroad, then someone was falling down in the marketing department. I don't do the Race Point's PR, but it seemed that might be something we'd find useful. I'd have to find out more... some other time.

Where would the inn—the house, then— have hidden the two sisters, and all the others who might have come through P'town?

I was trying to remember the cellar layout. In all my years at the Race Point, I'd never explored them, never felt a need to go down there. The big underground garage, yes, of course; that's where we'd constructed our inn's parade float during an extremely memorable Carnival. We didn't win the prize that year, but only—or so I assured myself—because the float had gotten blown up first.

I knew the kitchen had rooms and rooms of storage space down there, along with the sommelier's wine cellar, and who knew what else… But it might not even have been the cellars. I didn't know why that was where my mind had gone first. What else didn't I know about the inn? Were there false doors, hidden passageways I didn't know about?

This felt totally insane. "Are you sure?" I asked Jordan, realizing how lame my words were even as I spoke them. *Nice, Riley. Accuse the woman of lying. If she wasn't sure, why would she have said it? Are you sure you have a brain left?*

Jordan shrugged. "About the ghost? Of course not. Though honestly—I'd like to believe it. I don't know yet what became of Sarah."

"Yet?"

She nodded vigorously. I had a feeling she was grateful to be talking about ghosts, about anything other than the crushing loss she'd just experienced. "I haven't read everything, yet, I brought it all here with me. We were planning on staying an extra week after Women's Week was over, so I could read the material here, in situ as it were, and maybe meet with some local historians." I spared a thought for the much-beloved and very-much-missed historian Richard Olson. He'd have helped her, for sure, but not without a tart word or two to say about—well, everything.

Jordan was still talking. "So no, I don't know about what happened to her. Not yet. I haven't found it in Callie's writing; but I haven't been through it all yet, either. Maybe the journey was too much for her. Maybe she fell ill here. Maybe she stayed, though that seems a little farfetched."

"Well, in any case, *you're* welcome to stay," I said to Jordan.

She looked up at me. "Believe it or not, you can check, we actually do have reservations here, at the Race Point Inn, for next week. We were going to stay on. We were going to take our time, get to know the town." She smiled. "I might not have been born except for the role Provincetown played in my family's past."

There were voices behind us and I recognized Allie McDonald, the maid of honor at the wedding, who'd been my point of contact through all the planning. "I'm going to have to go talk to this person," I said to Jordan.

She nodded. "There's probably something I ought to be doing," she said.

"If they need you, they'll come for you," I said.

I was speaking from experience.

6

It's almost a guarantee: whenever my life gets chaotic—which, granted, seems to happen with more regularity than I like—and I can't add just one item or person to my dance card, my mother calls.

She didn't disappoint. The wedding was halfway over, the two brides sliding rings on each other's fingers, when I felt my phone vibrate. I was standing at the back of the patio next to Jordan, and I murmured an excuse and slipped back as far as the outdoor tiki bar. I didn't recognize the number. "Sydney Riley," I said crisply.

"I knew you wouldn't answer if you knew it was me."

I sighed. "Ma. This isn't the best time."

"It's never the best time. That's why I borrowed Andrea's phone. Andrea Richardson? You remember her? I borrowed her phone so you wouldn't have an excuse to not talk to me."

My mother was getting devious. That couldn't be a good sign. "What is it?"

"What is what?"

I tamped down several responses. *Breathe, Riley, breathe. Just breathe.* "What is it you called about, Ma?"

"Well, if I *must* have a reason to call my own daughter, then it's to point out that it's October now."

Do other mothers and daughters have conversations like this? Or am I just lucky? "I'm aware of that," I said, as calmly as I could. I signaled the bartender, and when he came over, I covered the phone for a moment. "Shot of Jameson's," I muttered to him. Conversations with my mother can't be accompanied by wine: I had to bring out the heavy artillery.

"Well," my mother was saying, "I'm just saying, it's not your dreadful *season* anymore, is it? And it's been forever since you've been up to see us, even though we really are close. You know our neighbor Adele Lorrimore? You remember her; she had that surgery a couple of years back, and we had to look after her dog. Remember that? Well, Adele's daughter

Barbara lives in New York City, and she sees *her* every *month*."

Adele Lorrimore's daughter Barbara was a hedge fund manager and probably had a private plane to take her to New Hampshire. And Adele herself was chronically unwell, whereas my mother has the constitution of a horse and will probably outlive us all. But I knew better than to mention any of that to her. "Ma, I'm right in the middle of Women's Week," I said.

"Women's Week? Never heard of it," she said, dismissing the concept.

Just because I could, I said, "It's a theme week for lesbians." All right, so I play the game, too. Sue me.

"I wish you didn't always have to parade all that so-called diversity in my face," my mother said a little plaintively. *So-called?* "It's all well and good for you to live with lesbians, but you don't have to actually talk about them. Your father and I respect your opinions, but, Sydney, we expect the same courtesy from you."

My mother has never in her life respected an opinion that ran counter to hers. I knew better than to mention that, too. "All it means is I have to be here, working," I said. "I have to be here for all the theme weeks. There's always a wedding or two going on."

She wasn't finished with her opinion. "It's a good thing you're going out with *that man*, otherwise I'd start to wonder if you hadn't turned lesbian yourself," she said darkly.

Breathe, Riley. Just breathe. I took a deep breath to steady myself. "Ma, there are so many things wrong with that sentence, I can't even begin to talk about them," I said. "Anyway, I have four more weddings this week."

She was undeterred. I have yet to meet anyone or anything that can deter my mother. "All women, I suppose," she said. "Marrying each other." She made it sound like one of the dark arts.

"That's right."

There was a very long pause, during which the bartender brought my shot and I did it. With alacrity. I waited. Eventually my mother would see she wasn't getting anywhere with the "so-called" diversity thing and try a different tack.

She didn't disappoint. "Well, good. One week. That means at the *end* of the week, you'll be free," she said.

"That's right," I said. "And I'm taking my vacation and going to Boston." With any luck, the fall would continue to stretch out beautiful and mild, and the trees on Boston Common would still be glorious.

Ali, of course, was *always* glorious.

A loud sniff. "You'd rather spend your time with *him*—"

"That's right."

"—than with your own flesh and blood."

Oh, goodie. The flesh-and-blood argument. "Ma," I said, "he's my boyfriend. Of course I want to spend my time off with him."

"It's not," said my mother, "as if he were your husband, or anything."

And there it was. We'd drilled down to the core of the problem and the centerpiece of every conversation we'd had for the past who-knew-how-many years. My mother wanted a wedding. My wedding. Specifically she wanted my wedding to one of the sons of her myriad friends, all of whom—to hear her—were handsome, wealthy, eligible, and absolutely panting to be with me.

All of whom were also Caucasian.

This wasn't my first rodeo. I'd already endured several—what am I saying, at least ten—of my mother's transparent attempts to marry me off, and had found the gentlemen in question to be as averse to the idea as I was. When

I started a relationship with Ali, she nearly went into shock.

He didn't come from New Hampshire. Cardinal sin.

Ali, accustomed to occasionally being the target of phobias, was philosophical about it. "She just has to get used to the idea," he said.

"She shouldn't have to get used to the idea!"

"In an ideal world, no," he conceded. "But that's not where we live, *cara*."

Ali and I been together for several years now, and my mother had made the apparently-to-her gigantic leap from "that Arab man" to just "that man."

We didn't have much common ground on the topic. I thought she could try harder. She thought I could get a different boyfriend.

I cleared my throat and held my empty shot glass up to the bartender. "Ma," I began, and she headed me off at the pass. "We haven't spent any time with you in almost a *year*," she pointed out. "I'd like to think you can fit us into your busy schedule more often than that."

Last Christmas my brain had short-circuited and in a moment of sheer insanity I'd invited my parents to Provincetown for the holidays. Worse still, they'd come. And even worse than that, I'd come pretty close to getting killed just a few hours before they arrived. I wasn't sure exactly why my mother would want to repeat that experience.

The bartender filled my glass again, I nodded my thanks, and polished it off. I was not, but not, going to promise her anything. Thanksgiving was on the not-so-distant horizon. She was going to ask me about Thanksgiving next; I'd put money on it. I wanted to spend it at the inn, with Ali. Damn it, I was *going* to spend it at the inn, with Ali. That was that.

There was a roar of delight from the patio and I looked over in time to see both brides launching their bouquets into the crowd of guests. Jordan was standing off to the side, hugging herself slightly, looking lost, and I came back to the moment. "Ma, I have to go."

"We haven't talked about Thanksgiving," she said quickly.

"No," I agreed. "We haven't. Gotta go, Ma, I'll talk to you soon." I clicked off before she could say anything else. Okay, so it was rude. But calling me on her friend's phone? Really?

For about the eightieth time I told myself I seriously needed to start work with a therapist. Maybe the same week I joined a gym.

Jordan looked relieved to see me. "Now what?" she asked.

"Nice wedding?"

She managed a smile. "Reminded me of ours," she said.

"You're married?" I was pretty sure Reggie had introduced Jordan as her partner.

"Don't look so surprised," she said. She actually looked a little surprised herself. "Canada legalized same-sex marriages before the United States did." She paused. "Though to be honest it took us a while. We've been together twelve years, but only got married about a year and a half ago. Reggie wanted to."

"I was just surprised because you don't wear a ring," I said. Of course Canada was ahead of us in marriage equality. From where I was sitting, Canada was ahead of us in most things.

"Reggie did," said Jordan. She held up both hands: no rings, no bracelet, not even a watch. "I have a skin condition," she said. "Metal irritates it."

I nodded, scarcely paying attention. "Let's get a drink," I suggested. The wedding party was all busy with champagne; only a few had gone to the tiki bar for something stronger, but even they were taking the drinks back down to the patio; there was no one at the bar. "I'll give Julie a call," I said. "Find out what's going on with the investigation."

Jordan looked relieved. "I was going to ask," she admitted.

"More Jameson's?" the bartender asked as I took my same seat again, Jordan perching next to me. I shook my head. "There are some extra bottles of champagne in the fridge," I told him. It wasn't great champagne—it never is, when you buy in quantity—but it wasn't terrible, either. I always ordered a couple of extras to have on hand; if the wedding party didn't need them, we could always use them.

"You got it." He opened one, expertly, absorbing the pressure of the cork in his bar towel, and poured us each a glass. I found Julie's icon on my phone and pressed it. "Hey, Julie, it's—"

"Where is she?" The voice was loud enough for both Jordan and the bartender to hear. Hell, the voice was loud enough for them to hear all the way to Long Point.

I glanced at Jordan. "She's with me at the inn."

"I've been calling her." It was still loud enough for me to not have to interpret. I looked at Jordan. She shrugged. "I didn't bother recharging it," she said.

"Her phone's off," I told Julie.

"I *know* her phone's off! What do you think I was just saying?"

"She can't be expected to remember things like that. She's in shock," I said, as soothingly as I could. "And we didn't know you were looking for her." What I really wanted to do was slap Julie around. Less than twenty-four hours after the dinner and Reggie's demise called for, I thought, a little more delicacy than she was showing.

"Stay right where you are. You hear me, Sydney? I'm coming over." She disconnected.

I looked at Jordan. She shrugged. "She's coming over," we said in unison.

I took a sip of champagne. A couple of wedding guests wandered over and sat at the bar, nodding to us, engaging the bartender in conversation. The sun was slanting low and the air was cooling rapidly; soon we'd all have to go inside. The wedding party had one of the dining rooms reserved for dinner and dancing, but Martin the maître d' was taking care of that part of the revels.

I wasn't needed for the wedding. What that meant was there was time for a little sleuthing instead.

Julie must have been right around the corner, because she appeared suddenly on the patio, standing just behind Jordan's shoulder. "Ms. Bellefort," she said, a little grimly.

Jordan started, coughing on the champagne she'd just drunk. Julie was impassive. "Are we celebrating?"

"It was my idea," I said. "Left over from the wedding." I gestured around us, where the revelers were just starting to trickle back into the inn. "Would you like a glass?"

She glared at me but didn't bother answering. "Ms. Bellefort, I have a few more questions for you."

Before Jordan could answer, I leaned over. "For pity's sake, Julie," I said, "Don't make her go down to the station. She's been through enough as it is."

Julie looked like she'd just as soon deck me as agree with me, but she usually looks like that. To my surprise and relief she climbed onto the stool next to Jordan. "Cranberry and soda," she said crisply to the bartender, and then turned back to us.

Jordan wasn't waiting. "Have you found out who killed Reggie?" she asked.

Julie looked at me, and I just raised my eyebrows in a well-*did*-you? sort of expression. At least, that was what I was aiming for.

"Not yet," she said to Jordan. "The state police will be wanting another formal statement from you."

"So it *is* homicide," I said. The police chief wouldn't call the Staties in unless he was sure. They'd already spoken to Jordan; if they wanted something more formal, it wasn't to justify their expenses.

She gave me a quelling look, but answered. "Yes," she said, and glanced at Jordan. "I'm very sorry," she said, gently.

"How?"

Julie took a second to think about it. "Someone strangled your friend," she said at length. "You can talk with the medical examiner, and in fact you'll have to, but from what I could see, Dr. Sanborn had a significant contusion on the back of her head. I think what happened was she was hit from behind and knocked out before being dragged into the bushes and strangled." She was watching Jordan for a reaction. I wondered if anyone passed out at this point in the conversation.

Julie took pity on her. "That means she was unconscious, you see," she said gently. "She wasn't aware of what was happening to her. Chances are she didn't feel anything. I don't know if that helps."

"Yes," said Jordan quietly. "Yes, it does. Thank you."

Julie sipped her cranberry spritz, still looking at Jordan. "And I have to ask you again, can you think of anyone who would have wanted to hurt Dr. Sanborn?"

Jordan shook her head. "This is our first time in the States," she said, frustration in her voice. "Except for Thea, Reggie didn't know anybody here. Well, and Billy."

"Billy?"

"My manager," said Jordan. "He came down with us from Canada. Making contacts, networking, all that sort of thing. This seemed to be too good an opportunity for him to pass up, getting to meet some of the American musicians…" Her voice trailed off.

"I met Billy," I said. "Nice man." I didn't know if it was true or not, but I felt I should say something about him. Blond man? Young man?

"Last name?" asked Julie.

"Thompson," said Jordan. "Billy Thompson."

"Where is Mr. Thompson now?" asked Julie.

"Probably at a bar somewhere," said Jordan. She sounded exhausted.

"He was going to go talk to the venues where Jordan was scheduled to perform," I told Julie. "You know, cancelling her appearances."

She wrote that down and looked at Jordan again. "And you? Do you know anyone else here?"

Jordan looked around her a little wildly, as if expecting someone to pop up if she mentioned their name. "Some of the musicians," she said finally. "They've been to some of the same festivals as me, up in Canada. Women's music in North America is like a club; we're always running into each other."

"That reminds me," said Julie, who never needed to be reminded of anything in her life. "Why haven't you come here before this? It seems you have quite a following."

Jordan hesitated. "To be honest? The United States doesn't have that grand a reputation, eh? We've really never been on the same page politically, and—well, all right,

106

here's the thing, there's something about going somewhere to perform, it says something. It's like a seal of approval even if it isn't articulated that way. And Reggie's a real homebody. But then, this time, I had a reason to come to Provincetown anyway, some research I'm going on my ancestors, so Billy said he could get me the gig for Women's Week, so we decided to make a holiday of it. There were some people here I wanted to meet. Billy arranged it all. He hooked up with the accompanist, Jon…"

"Richardson," I supplied. Ali and I sometimes went to piano bar at Tin Pan Alley or the Crown & Anchor to hear Jon.

"Right," said Jordan. "Richardson. But mostly it was for the project, to learn more about my great-great-grandmother."

Julie wasn't interested in ancestral research "And yet there must be a reason she was killed," she said, her voice level. "Someone went to a fair bit of trouble to lure her, and her specifically, out of that room."

"How did that work, anyway?" I demanded. "Knowing there were two doctors in the room, and getting Thea out first, that timing had to be just right, didn't it? And how did anybody know there were two doctors in the first place?"

"What do you mean, getting Thea out first?" asked Jordan.

Julie was giving me The Look again. "She has a right to know," I pointed out.

Julie sighed. "A guest apparently fell and injured themselves in the lobby," she said. "Her companion—her son, I think it was—was worried about her, and the front desk sent someone to request Dr. Madison's assistance."

"The complete other end of the inn from the banquet hall," I put in. "So it would take her a while to get there, and then to tape the guest's ankle, deal with the problem, tell her what to do to take care of herself, and then the long walk back to the banquet room."

"I was not unaware of that fact," said Julie coolly. The bartender put her drink in front of her and she took a sip, automatically, without looking at the drink or at him. "Soon after Dr. Madison left the room, there was an announcement a staff member had cut themselves, and the person was asking for a doctor."

Jordan nodded. "I remember that," she said. "Vaguely. It didn't really register, I'd never have thought it would involve Reggie, we're just visitors here."

"Normally it wouldn't," said Julie. "That's why the call to Dr. Madison becomes so important. We're looking into it."

Jordan looked from one of us to the other. "And then what?" she asked. "What happened to Reggie?"

Julie took a deep breath. "We don't have a clear picture of it yet," she said. "I'd be guessing—"

"Please," said Jordan. "Please guess." She sounded about five years old.

"So think about the room where the buffet was set up," said Julie. "Most of the food was being ferried back and forth from the kitchen on carts. Behind where the line was set up, there's a coat closet—a pretty large one. There's also a bar set up in the buffet room, but it wasn't being used last night, you'll remember the cash bar was in the same room as the banquet tables."

"The coat room?" I asked.

She shrugged. "I'm guessing yes. Like I said, it would be quick. And there's a fire exit behind that." She sighed. "That place, the Provincetown Inn—there are more ways in and out of it than any other building in town. Some of the guest rooms open to the outside.

Dining rooms, banquet halls, everything opens up."

"To catch the sea breeze," I said. I hadn't thought of it that way. If you wanted to slip in and out of someplace and have lots of options, it was a perfect place. "Still, it was taking a big chance, wasn't it? That a staff person would be there loading up dishes to take back to the kitchen? That one of the guests would come back for an extra serving of pumpkin pie?"

"Apparently it was worth the risk," said Julie. She was watching Jordan, who was shaking her head. "But why?" Jordan asked. "Why was it worth the risk? No one here knew Reggie—except for Billy, of course. And Thea."

"Right," said Julie. She wasn't interested in Jordan's manager; he hadn't been at the dinner. "They went to medical school together, Dr. Sanborn and Dr. Madison, right? Where was that?" She'd probably already asked Thea, I thought.

Jordan said, "Dalhousie," as though her mind were somewhere else. She saw our blank looks. "Dalhousie University Faculty of Medicine," she amplified. "It's in Halifax."

"Why did *Thea* go there?" I asked. That part hadn't occurred to me. Why would she go to Canada? If I'd given it any thought at all, I'd have inferred Thea's roots were in the Caribbean somewhere.

Jordan slanted me a look. "She was seeing someone who lived in Halifax," she said. "Dating him, I mean. Involved romantically. A politician. He was a member of parliament for years, so there was no question of him going anywhere else, so she moved to Halifax to be with him."

"Him?" I asked, sure I hadn't heard her right.

She smiled sadly. "Thea tends to fall in love with people, not genders," she said. Something told me it wasn't that simple, but this was neither the time nor the place to pursue it. "She and Simon were an item for at least three years, if I'm remembering correctly."

"What happened?"

She shrugged. "He wanted a family; she wanted to be a doctor. He didn't want to wait around. He's still an MP, has three children and a very blonde wife." She paused. "And Thea's a doctor."

Julie wasn't going to let us hijack the conversation. "And Dr. Sanborn didn't know anyone at the dinner besides Dr. Madison?" How many different ways was she going to ask the same thing?

Jordan shook her head. "Why would she?" she asked rhetorically. She inhaled, impatient. "Look, she worked at a community health center, eh? It's all neighborhood people, low-income residents, people we know. What Americans would she meet there? She sang in the choir at church. What Americans would she meet there? She's on the board of the Africville Heritage Trust. What Americans would she meet there? All that matters to Reggie is her community. She'd be happy never leaving Halifax. She didn't know any Americans. She came here for me. Because of me." She dashed at her eyes. "She didn't even want to come, not really. I persuaded her she needed a holiday, time to recharge. She works too much. She doesn't have to, but she does. Did." She took a deep breath. "She didn't know any Americans," she repeated.

I wasn't listening: there was that name I'd caught before: Africville. Intriguing. I wanted to know more, so see how it fit in to the women's narratives. *Again, Riley, not the time or the place.*

"So," said Julie, "maybe it wasn't an American."

We sat with the thought for a moment. I shook my head to clear it. Too many questions. "No. If it was a Canadian, why would they wait until Reggie was in the States to go after her?" I demanded. "That doesn't make sense. There were probably a million opportunities in Halifax. It's a city, it's easier to blend in, there wasn't just that one-off chance of finding her alone. Why follow her here?" It made as much sense, I thought, as my first reaction to hearing P'town was a stop on the Underground Railroad: it was a long way out here, to the tip of the Cape, to land's end. You had to really want something badly to be willing to take the journey—and the risk. There's only one road out of this town, which didn't sound like great odds for feeling safe about committing a crime. Unless the killer, like the conductors, was planning to leave by sea.

But even *that* was more complicated today than it was when Callie and Sarah were making their secret journey. We had the harbormasters. We had the Coast Guard.

Julie said, "For some reason, this was the only time and place that mattered. If we can figure that out, maybe we're a step closer to putting the who to the how and the what." She paused, thinking. "Who knew you were coming to Provincetown?" she asked Jordan. "When did you make the arrangements?"

Jordan thought for a moment. "I hadn't really planned to come," she said, thinking it through. "I only really started reading the journals, the letters, last year."

"Journals?" Julie's pen was poised.

"The research I was talking about," said Jordan. "My great-great-grandmother came through here as a fugitive slave on the Underground Railroad. I spent most of last winter tracing her back to the plantation—there are lists online, stuff like that—and then Provincetown caught my eye. I don't know how long she stayed here, but she was definitely here, she names it in her journal. And I knew about Women's Week, of course, it's famous. So I asked Billy to see if he could get me in." She paused. "Reggie was more likely to want to come if I was performing," she said. "And I've never been to the States, I didn't want to come alone. So we thought—I thought—we could make it all happen at once." Another pause. "Reggie loved to hear me sing," she said, wistful.

"So sometime last year your manager made the arrangements?"

Jordan nodded. "By Christmas," she said. "Certainly by Christmas."

"And who knew?"

She shrugged. "Me. Billy. Reggie. People at the clinic, she had to get someone lined up to substitute for her. People at our church, they'd worry if we just disappeared. She probably told people at the museum where she's on the board. But it was no secret. Billy probably told tons of people, he likes impressing the fans. Plus, it's on my website. It was in my newsletter. Probably all over social media."

Julie glared at me, as if the social media exposure were somehow my responsibility. "*I'm* not her manager," I pointed out.

Her eyes went past me, out to the locked wrought-iron gate that kept our pool and patio and tiki bar as guests-only enclaves. There were two men standing there. Wearing suits.

In P'town, if you're wearing a suit, you're either getting married or you're a woman doing drag. Those are the only possible reasons.

Unless, of course, you're the state police.

7

Mike showed the cops and Jordan into the lounge and closed the door on them for some privacy. I wasn't worried: I was pretty sure that anything Jordan knew, we already knew. I just wanted to be around when they were finished; I had a feeling she'd be a little worse for wear.

"You like her, don't you?" Julie's eyes were following the group as they left. Behind us, the wedding party had gone inside, and the outdoor lights were already coming on. I hate that about October, how it seems we start diving headlong into early darkness. Every day is shorter than the last.

"I do like her," I acknowledged. "She's an interesting person with an interesting story. She's nice. And she's really holding up well with everything going on. I'd have gone to pieces by now if that had been Ali." I glanced over, caught her smile. "What?"

"If anyone tried that with Ali," she said, "they'd be the ones ending up in the bushes."

Probably true, but I didn't want to think about it. I'm not thrilled with my boyfriend's job. I'm not thrilled that he deals with unspeakably violent people on a daily basis. I hate it when he goes undercover—and about thirty percent of his job seems to involve going undercover—when I don't know for days or weeks whether he's even alive. I hate almost everything about it, actually.

On the other hand, he's making a difference in the world. He's saving lives. He's reuniting families. He's changing attitudes. Me? I facilitate weddings.

Julie was watching me, amused. She slapped the bar as though finalizing something. "All right," she said, turning away. "I'm off. Stay in touch."

"Julie?"

She turned back. "Yeah?"

"Thanks for letting me in, like this, today." It wasn't her usual modus operandi, and I was grateful. And not about to rock the boat by asking why. Maybe because I hadn't actually been the one to find the dead body, this time around? "I appreciate it."

"Don't get used to it," she said.

I walked slowly back through the gate and into the inn. It felt unexpectedly warm inside, which showed just how cold it was getting. October announcing itself in no uncertain terms.

Mike was sitting at my desk in my cubbyhole. "Hi, there," I said. "Please make yourself at home. It's not as if you had a whole big office to yourself... oh, wait! You *do* have a whole big office to yourself."

"I couldn't find you. How do you make sense of your calendar?"

"I think the point is that *I* can make sense of it," I said. "No one else needs to." He didn't move. "Can I help you with something, Mike?"

"I have a guy in my office wants to arrange a wedding."

"And you've decided to try and do it on your own? What, my job isn't in the budget anymore?"

"I was just checking what dates you had open," he said, a little defensively.

I sighed. I had to wait for Jordan, anyway. And my plans for dinner revolved, as usual, around removing something from my freezer and transferring it to the microwave oven. "Okay," I said. "Where is he?"

Mike perked right up. "In my office," he said.

"Ah, yes. That one. The one you have that I don't." But I was smiling; I couldn't help it. I can't stay irritated with him for long.

"Lead on, MacDuff," I suggested.

Outside the door, Mike checked himself. "I should warn you," he said. "He's not the usual."

"Who is?" Provincetown doesn't have a "usual." We go strictly by the assumption that the wilder, the better, but even with that knowledge, the visitor was a little odd.

The beard was what you noticed first, and it was impressive, well-tended and well past the gentleman's collar. The eyes behind the glasses held a definite twinkle.

He stood up when I came in and took my hand. "Miss Riley. A pleasure, it's truly a pleasure to meet you," he said. The accent didn't disappoint.

Mike said, "This is Howard Carter, Sydney. He's interested in arranging a wedding."

I smiled. "Congratulations, Mr. Carter. Won't you sit down?" I perched on the other guest chair, my notebook at the ready. I didn't know if Mike had intended for us to meet there and then, but I was taking advantage of the office space. Some of us don't actually *have* office space.

He waited until I was seated before taking his place back in the chair. "Please, Miss Riley, ma'am, you have to call me Howard," he said. I must have been imagining the twinkle in his eye; but it was there in his voice. "Maybe even Howie, once we get to know each other."

I glanced at Mike, who was settling in behind his desk. He gave me a theatrical shrug. "Okay, Howard," I said. "You can call me Sydney. Tell me about your wedding plans."

"Oh, Miss Sydney, nothing as grand as plans yet, no siree," he said. "That's where y'all come in, isn't it? Planning the wedding?"

I took a deep breath. I didn't risk looking at Mike again; he was probably struggling to keep a straight face. "Of course," I said encouragingly. "Howard, when would you like to get married?"

"There you go," he said with satisfaction. "Right to the point. I like that. I like a woman who gets down to brass tacks. There are a lot of women who don't, I can tell you that, yes, ma'am. Women from my neck of the woods like to obfuscate. They view conversation as a sport. But never mind that, now. I have to admit to you, about the date? It's been a point of contention between the lovely lady in question, my charming fiancée, and myself. Yes, sir. A true point of contention."

I had a feeling I'd stepped into a rehearsal of something Tennessee Williams-y. The accent, the cadence of Howard's voice: Southern Gothic at its best. Even in the chill of a New England October evening, the dense heat, the swamps and Spanish moss of the South seemed for a moment to fill the room. I blinked, and I was back sitting beside a middle-aged man whose mannerisms had to be a century out of date. "Mr. Carter—"

"Howard, ma'am."

"Howard," I said firmly. "The date is unfortunately the first thing we need to ascertain. Are you thinking of sometime in the spring? Or next summer?" *Give me a ballpark month to work with, Howard.*

"Spring," he said, nodding. "Lydia—that's the lady in question, and believe me when I tell you that she truly is a lady—well, she is partial to springtime. Yes, ma'am, she is."

"I see." *And where is said lady?* "Generally we like to talk to both parties," I said. And generally, when it's a male/female wedding, it's the bride who's calling the shots. There was a lot about this situation that had me curious.

He laughed at that, almost a bark. "Of course! Of course! She had some business—" he pronounced it *bidness*—"to take care of. In New York City, if you can believe that! These women executives, you just can't keep them down, now can you? She's joining me here in a couple of days, my Lydia is. She's flying up from the city, I believe that's how you people refer to it, as the city, am I wrong, Miss Sydney? I came up first, to get the lay of the land, yes, ma'am."

Mike said, "Mr. Carter's staying with us for a week, Sydney."

"Howard, sir," corrected the guest. "And that's right. Take a look at this charming little town of yours while we make the wedding arrangements." He was patting his pockets, trying to find something. "Thought I'd put it here…"

There was a pause and then he withdrew a pill container from an inner pocket. "Just a moment, truly sorry to be an inconvenience, if you could get me a glass of water…"

I looked at Mike. He answered, obliquely, "Howard's in the Harry Kemp suite." No inflection in his voice, but he didn't need emphasis: Harry Kemp (named for a street that was in turn named for a famous Provincetown poet) was our largest, most expensive suite. Howard Carter was Someone Important, at least as far as the Race Point Inn was concerned.

I fetched the water, and waited while Howard downed the pill. "Bit of a condition," he said, apologetically. "The ticker. Not as hale and hearty as I used to be."

"None of us is," said Mike smoothly.

"Are you all right?" I asked.

He nodded. "Just a precaution, Miss Sydney, ma'am, just a precaution." Another bark of laughter. "Have a couple more things to get done before I pack it all in. Like gettin' married. Never thought the day would come, I can tell you that. But startin' to take the long view. Look at my legacy. What I'm leaving behind."

I looked at Mike uncertainly, but his face gave nothing away. "Well, welcome," I said to Howard. "We're delighted you're here. Why don't we plan on meeting once—um—Lydia arrives? Then we can set some dates and get a sense of how we can help you plan the perfect wedding."

He beamed. I thought for a moment he was going to slap his thigh, but he managed to contain his delight. "Well, then, Miss Sydney, I'll say good-night for now, and I'll look forward to speaking with you later."

I stood up with him and shook his hand. "It was nice to meet you, Howard."

Mike said, "I'll see you out."

Howard paused at the door. "Heard there was a problem last night," he said. "Somewhere else in town? Another hotel? Woman got herself killed?"

I stiffened; Reggie hadn't gotten herself killed, someone had killed her. Semantics matter. Maybe it was a Southern phrasing I didn't know. Mike's eyes were telling me to let it go. "Yes," I said. "Over at the Provincetown Inn."

"Terrible thing, just terrible. I just don't know what this world is coming to, no, sir, I don't. When a nice girl can't have a dinner in peace. Well, thank you for your time. I'll just nip over to the bar for a few minutes, wet my whistle as they say."

"Have a good evening," said Mike formally, and closed the door behind him. He turned and looked at me. "Well, and here you thought Carnival was the only time we got the odd ducks in here," he said.

"At least we know he's not the killer," I said.

"Oh? How's that?"

"Imagine that man hanging out with a group of lesbians," I suggested.

"The mind," agreed Mike, "boggles."

And yet I wondered, all the same, how it was that Howard Carter had known the death was at dinner.

Jordan was apparently still talking to the state police. I wondered what about. I avoided the main bar so I wouldn't have to deal with Howard, and picked up a glass of Côtes du Rhône from the restaurant bar and retreated with it to my cubbyhole behind Reception to wait for her. I had a feeling she wouldn't want to be alone, not after what was surely a need-lessly formal—and second—interrogation.

I flipped through my date book, noting a few possible options for Howard and Lydia, but I was tired and my mind wandered. If I were going to commit a crime such as murder, I mused, I actually couldn't choose a better spot than an inn, especially one as large and spread out as the Provincetown Inn (though, honestly, the Race Point would work pretty well, too). Even in October, especially during a nice October, the inn is full of people.

The sheer size of the Provincetown Inn invites intrigue. There's a bar and restaurant that are both open to the public. There are function rooms. There are guest rooms on two floors and in three wings. Everyone walks through going one way or another; the reception area is tucked off to one side and its staff are generally busy and not paying attention to what is happening in the lobby, noticing who is coming and going—and even if they were paying attention, they wouldn't recognize anyone out of place, simply because no one looks out of place. You wouldn't even have to be brisk or look like you knew where you were going. Long gone where the days when you'd have to go to Reception to pick up your key.

The guest and her son, the people who'd asked for help, must have done so deliberately, getting the desk clerk's attention and making an issue of it. I'd be willing to bet good money that someone mentioned the word liability—which rendered instant results. But someone knew to send for Thea, specifically: they knew she was there. Who knew that? Dinner guests don't check in at the front desk.

What that said to me was there was someone involved in this who knew Provincetown and the workings of Women's Week very well indeed.

***

Jordan looked exhausted. There was a gray tinge to her skin, and her eyes were bloodshot.

"They kept asking if Reggie and I had any problems," she said. We stood together in the lobby watching the police leave. She turned to me. "I could use a drink."

What we didn't need to do was run into Howard, I decided. I didn't analyze why I was avoiding him; later, I would remember that, and wonder what voice had been whispering in my ear. "Let's go out," I suggested. Strangers and Saints was right down the street, and what with the wedding and all, neither of us had eaten anything. "We can get a late supper."

"I'm not hungry," Jordan protested.

"You will be," I predicted. "Besides, they do amazing small plates. We'll find something to share." Like the Moroccan carrots, Ali's favorite, or the Brussels sprout hash. And a glass of—something. At this point I wasn't sure it mattered, I'd had enough strange things to drink all day that one more wasn't going to mean anything.

We sat at the bar and ordered a bottle of wine. "It's an odd name for a restaurant," Jordan commented. "What does it mean?"

"You're a history buff, you'll enjoy this," I said. Lubricating small talk, I thought, just what Jordan needed. Something that had nothing to do with murder. "You know the Mayflower came here first, right? To Provincetown?" She nodded, and I waited until the wine was poured and we'd each taken a sip. "There were one hundred and two passengers on the Mayflower," I said. "We think of them all as Pilgrims, with a capital P, but actually less than half were part of a religious group. The passengers were split into two groups—the Separatists, or saints, and the rest of the passengers, who were called strangers." I sketched air-quotes around each noun.

"I didn't know that."

I shrugged. "Most people don't. History isn't taught very well in schools." I glanced at her. "Maybe you do better in Canada." There's nothing like hanging out with someone from another country to see the deficiencies in yours. "Anyway, the Strangers were described pretty much as common people. They were the tradesmen, craftsmen, skilled workers, laborers, indentured servants, that sort of thing. Working people. The Saints weren't particularly nice to them—no one started out here on equal footing, no matter what the Compact and the Founding Fathers would have us believe."

"Don't I know," said Jordan. She caught my look and shrugged. "I've been researching American history on the South, eh?" she reminded me. "Those Founding Fathers owned slaves."

Like Callie and Sarah, I thought. And congratulated myself again on staying away from Howard. Something told me Jordan and Howard weren't exactly going to hit it off. Something told me plantations were firmly planted in his family tree, just as they were in Jordan's, though their respective ancestors had experienced the environment quite differently.

On the other hand, she'd introduced the topic of history, and I was curious. "Tell me more about your research," I said. "And about Africville. I have to say I'm intrigued by the name."

Jordan smiled, a little wanly. "It's Reggie who should have told you about that," she said. "Oh, we're both on the board and all, but for me, it was just a pastime. Something we could do together. For her—it was a passion." She sipped her wine. "So, Africville," she said. "What Africville is really about is everything that's wrong with racism, and everything that's right with making amends."

The food arrived. I'd have to remember to tell Ali that I'd had the carrots without him. Make him want to come visit. "Do you mind? Telling me?"

"This is delicious! So, anyway—Canada just loves to brag about how Nova Scotia was the last stop on the underground railroad. We even had national television propaganda program that showed happy slaves popping out of the furniture they'd been smuggled in on, and finding a new life in the Great White North." The way she said them, I could tell the words were capitalized. "But not everyone knows what a horrible time some of the former slaves—and their descendants—had once they got there, where they ended up living, how white people treated them." She paused; I couldn't tell if it was for the drama or not. "Not everyone knows about Africville."

It sounded totally ominous. I was pretty sure that was on purpose. She was a decent storyteller, Jordan. She paused a little longer, then went on. "Africville was a primarily Black community on the outskirts of Halifax. Right on the water, a truly pretty place. The first community records date back to 1848, and it continued to exist for a century and a half after that."

"Wait," I said. "1848? Isn't that when your ancestor escaped from—here?"

Jordan nodded and took a sip of wine. "She arrived three years after Africville was founded," she said. "She was one of the community's pioneers. She helped build Africville. Eventually there were shops, a school, a post office, and the Seaview United Baptist Church; the church was Africville's spiritual and social center."

"It sounds—" I'd almost said "idyllic," but that didn't work.

"It was what it was," said Jordan, taking pity on me. "People cared about each other. You don't see that much anymore." Except in Provincetown, I thought, but I didn't say anything. Jordan ticked a list off on her fingers. "There were two real challenges for the community: one was overt and sometimes violent racial discrimination, and number two was poverty. Africville was worse off than any city slums, to tell you the truth. Halifax wouldn't provide anything: there was no sewage, no access to clean water, no garbage disposal. The people paid taxes and took pride in their homes, but when they asked for services, nothing happened. Over time the city built a ring around Africville that made things worse: an infectious disease hospital, a prison, and a dump. The hospital just threw the bodies of patients who'd died straight into the dump. It was toxic. There was all sorts of disease."

"Sounds deliberate," I said.

She nodded. "It was," she said. "But generations lived there, generations toughed it out. It was their home. They were willing to pay the price to have their community. But the city was having none of it. They wanted to develop the land. They weren't going to say that upfront, so instead they tried to make it sound like they actually cared about the people. They claimed relocation would improve the standard of living for residents." She snorted. "Of course, they never actually *consulted* with the residents, asked them what they wanted; they didn't want to know what they wanted. It was irrelevant. So in 1964 they started moving people out." She took another swallow of wine.

"Wait," I said. "What do you mean, moving people out? They forced people to leave?"

"People who could prove they owned land were offered reasonable payment. Go figure what that meant. People without proof–and, come on, some residents didn't have deeds, even if their families had lived on the site for generations, no one thought they needed anything, it was their community–those people were given five hundred dollars. Even in the sixties, that was insulting. And impossible. Anyone who resisted was forcibly removed; there's a story of one woman taken out of her house in a city garbage truck. How is that for symbolism?"

"It's awful," I said.

Jordan nodded. "By 1970 it was all over," she said. "The last house was destroyed. Say what you will about segregation, the truth is, when the people of Africville were there, they were self-sufficient. They might not have had a lot of money, but they weren't on government assistance. They were trying to create a community, a real community, but the government had other priorities. So when they relocated people, everyone went on assistance and social housing—so what they were really doing was taking their dignity from them."

"I'm sorry," I said. "This must be so painful. Was *your* family relocated?"

She took a deep breath. "Mine, and Reggie's, too. That's how we met, you see: there's an organization for Africville descendants. We both went to a meeting. That was how it started between us." She paused "Her parents were relocated to a place called Hammond Plains. One day her father opened a letter. It was threatening to burn his house down if he and his family didn't leave. It was signed *from the white people of Hammond Plains*." She picked up a carrot slice on her fork, looked at it, set it down again. "Since then, Africville's become Reggie's passion, what she lives—what she lived for. Nowadays there's a park, and a museum with lots of consciousness-raising educational programs, and not long ago the bell from the church was returned there. It's become something to appreciate and identify with."

It was a sad story, I thought. "At least Callie never saw the destruction," I said, bringing the narrative home. "Was she happy there?"

Jordan smiled. "She was," she said. Talking about Africville had made her pensive; she lit up, though, when talking about Callie. "She taught literacy. She got married in the Baptist church, and she had five children. Four of them died young—I can't help but think it was of poverty, because even though she writes about diseases, diseases come out of poverty—but the oldest, my great-grandfather, survived. She named him Freeman, and she taught him to read and write." She smiled. "My grandmother went to Dalhousie University. I think Callie would have been beside herself."

"Such a shame Sarah couldn't have been with her," I said. I was looking at my glass of wine, twisting the stem between my fingers, mentally drifting; my day was catching up to me, I was close to hitting a wall. It took me a moment to realize Jordan hadn't responded. I looked up at her. There was something in her eyes, something smoldering and dangerous. "What? What is it, Jordan?"

"Sarah was lost at sea," she said, her voice steady.

"Yes," I said, not understanding. "You told me."

"Sarah was—we'd call it depressed. She'd been—hurt, at the plantation. Well, they all were, eh? But Sarah, she didn't get over it. So Callie says." She took a deep breath. "I think Sarah went off the side of the boat on purpose. Callie hints at it, never really comes out with it. Callie turned and Sarah just wasn't there anymore. She screamed and made them stop, but it was night, it was the ocean, they were under pressure to meet up with the Canadians, they couldn't find her."

"But she was so close to being free," I said. "Why would she want to kill herself? After everything they'd been through?"

"That is a good question," she said. "It's part of what I plan to find out."

But when I left her to head home to my apartment and my cat, I still wasn't sure what it was she was looking for.

8

Thursday dawned late, with rain coursing down my windows; the first half of Women's Week had been, it seemed, too good to last.

I had two weddings.

I was thinking about them as I ate a bowl of oatmeal and stared moodily out at the street. The later one wasn't a problem: it was scheduled to be inside, with a band and dancing, and I couldn't see anything that could go wrong there. Outside of the things that always go wrong with weddings, of course; there's a large margin of error there.

It was the three o'clock one that had me worried. I fumbled for my phone and checked the weather app. Not looking good.

Everyone is warned, of course; Provincetown's shoulder seasons, neither summer nor winter, can turn from one to the other in a minute. No celebration of any kind scheduled after October first or before June first comes without a Plan B, with Plan C preferably lurking not far away.

My three o'clock brides had met during a past Women's Week very specifically out on the Race Point Inn patio, one of them having taken advantage of the empty bower during an unseasonably warm afternoon to sit and read a book, the other wandering about passing time before the next organized event of the day, some sort of workshop. They had met at three o'clock. At that bower. They were determined that they should marry at three o'clock. At the bower. "It's our wedding, it will be perfect!" Glynnis, the reader, had assured me.

"But if it rains—"

"It won't, you'll see!"

That was either magical thinking or this woman could really control the clouds, in which case I wanted to hire her on the spot. As I rinsed my bowl and poured more coffee, the wind shifted and started throwing the rain up against the window instead. A step in the wrong direction. "This isn't looking good," I told Ibsen. He stared at me for a moment and went back to licking his paw, showing off what a Totally Calm Cat he could be in the face of disaster.

Ali called when I was just getting out of the shower. "*Cara.* I miss you."

"I miss you, too," I said. "I think my mother's gearing up to invite us for Thanksgiving."

"I don't think she believes I celebrate Thanksgiving."

"Yeah, true enough, that's why I thought I'd leave you and Ibsen here with some peanut butter while I go to New Hampshire," I said.

"Promises, promises."

I felt myself relaxing. Nothing could go seriously awry with Ali a phone call away. "It's raining," I informed him.

"Lucky girl. You have a wedding?"

"I have two, but only one outdoors. Maybe it'll clear by then." I was ready to start climbing on board the Magical Thinking Bus.

"Not according to the weather station," said my boyfriend prosaically. "Maybe they'll postpone." Yep: he was getting on board, too. "Any news on your homicide investigation?"

"The boys from South Yarmouth are here," I said. "They've already talked with Jordan twice. I don't get that—she was standing in front of a hundred people when Reggie was killed. Why they keep coming back to her—"

"Questioning her twice isn't quite the same as 'keep coming back to her', *cara*."

"No? Then what is it? Are they pulling a Columbo—oh, sir, just one last thing, it's just this one little thing that's still bothering me..." Ali and I had recently discovered the television crime series that had started before either of us was born, and loved the rumpled detective with his cigar and his offhanded approach to interrogating criminals. Ali maintained the every episode of Columbo was a study in detection. I just thought they were fun.

"When you question a number of people," Ali said, "sometimes you get information that contradicts something someone said earlier. Or that *builds* on what someone said earlier. Then you have to go back and get clarity. Plus, your friend Jordan knows more about the victim than anyone else there, so of course they're interested in talking to her. It's procedure, *cara*."

I was still feeling protective of Jordan. "Well, I don't like it," I said.

"Hmm," said Ali, whether in agreement or dismissal I didn't know. "Just do what you can for her. Oh, and *cara*?"

"Yes?"

"Please remember that there's probably still someone walking around there who's already killed once. Lock your doors. Pay attention to what's around you, especially if you plan to spend time with Jordan. I don't want anything happening to you."

"This seemed like a particularly specialized murder," I said. "Focused, you know? I can't think I'm in any danger."

"And we've all heard *that* song before."

I smiled; I had to smile. For all that I fret over the dangers inherent in Ali's job, I know he frets over the situations in which I often seem to entangle myself. Maybe the worry adds spice to our relationship, who knows?

Or maybe it just adds worry.

"So," I said carefully, "that thing you were saying about missing me…"

***

The first person I saw at the inn was Howard Carter, standing near the reception desk and looking just as elegant as he had the evening before. "Good morning, Miss Sydney," he said. If he'd been wearing his hat, no doubt he'd have swept it off to greet me.

"Hello, Howard," I said. I leaned over the reception desk. "Any messages for me?"

The kid staffing it was on the phone, but he shook his head.

"Thanks." I turned back to Howard. "Can I do anything for you? Were you waiting for me?"

"As a matter of fact, Miss Sydney, ma'am, I was."

There was a longish pause. *Okay. And you wanted to see me about…?* "How can I help you?"

"Well, you see, I was thinkin' about what you said last night. About setting a date right away for the wedding, not discussin' anything else, and so on. That took me a little by surprise, I have to admit, because I was hopin' you could be a little more helpful upfront. Of course, I didn't want to say anything in front of your manager, it's not my goal to get you in trouble, not at all. Nothing could be further from my mind, no, ma'am. So I thought you and me, we could have ourselves a little *tête-a-tête*"—he pronounced it tait-ah-tait—"without him knowin', and smooth things out before they get to be bigger things." He gave me a broad, bland smile. "If you see what I mean, ma'am."

I had no idea what he meant, but the kid at the desk was listening with obvious interest, and—how many times was I going to have to remind myself this week?—it was neither the time nor the place. "Howard," I said. "I don't know what's upset you about our conversation last night, but I'll be very happy to talk with you. Unfortunately, I have some things I need to see to first. If you'd like to make an appointment—"

"Now, see, that disappoints me, that does, ma'am." Had the be the cardinal Southern sin, that: interrupting. "Seein' as I'm staying in your *numero-uno* suite here, and your manager has been most accommodating with everything else…" His voice trailed off, delicately.

"My manager doesn't know my schedule," I said. "I'm afraid that I'm just a little distracted right now—" I don't usually get too annoyed with any of our guests. I was starting to feel annoyed with Howard Carter.

He must have been feeling the vibes, because he tried another tack. "I understand the lady is stayin' here, the one whose friend got killed the other night."

"Her *wife*," I said firmly.

"Is that who was killed?" he asked, and his hand suddenly went to his chest, and I remembered last night's pills. "Are you all right?" I asked, anxiously, not entirely sure if this was the polite Howard from last night experiencing a medical emergency or today's Howard pushing the boundaries. A glance at his face settled the question; his skin looked green. "Call the rescue squad!" I yelled at the kid at the desk, and put my arm around Howard. "Do you need a pill?" I asked. I could feel the tremor under my hand. "Come here, slowly, let's sit you down." We shuffled over to the stiff loveseat across from Reception. "They want to know what's wrong," said the kid.

"Heart attack," I said. I had no idea whether or not it was true, but they were the medical personnel, not me; let them diagnose him. "Tell them to hurry, damn it!"

"Don't have time for this," Howard was mumbling. "Get me Glenn or Mike," I said to the kid. "And some water. Get the water first!"

I turned back to Howard. "It's okay," I said soothingly. "We have all the time in the world. Just breathe." The advice I gave myself on a regular basis. I'm pretty much Anxiety Girl, jumping from zero to the sky is falling in ten seconds flat. I was doing it now. *Don't die on me, Howard.* "Breathe," I urged him again. "Help is coming."

"No time for this," he mumbled. "I have to get to the meeting…"

"No meeting for you," I said firmly. Maybe ever. "Forget about it. Help really is coming, Howard, just breathe for me."

Help came, first, in the shaggy person of Glenn, the inn's owner, bringing with him a glass of water and a concerned expression. "Mr. Carter," he said, sitting down on the other side of our patient. The loveseat shook a little, but held up, and I blessed its workmanship. The three of us were pretty damned crowded there, and Glenn is what we call a bear—a very large, very hairy gay man. If the loveseat hadn't held, we'd have *all* had a heart attack. "Do you want a sip of water? The rescue squad is on the way. Is there anything we can get you right now?"

"Do you need one of your pills?" I asked again, remembering.

Howard seemed to rally a little. He moistened his lips and then looked at me. "Seems you could find the time now," he said. "You could come to the meeting."

What meeting?

Glenn was looking at me oddly. "Howard, you're not a burden," I said desperately. I wasn't going to be anywhere close to forgiving myself if he died.

Mike came in through the front door, holding it open for two EMTs, who immediately shouldered their way past me and Glenn. Mike mouthed "what happened?" over their shoulders and I shrugged.

They were efficient. They talked to Howard in loud voices, and ended up bringing in a gurney from the ambulance. A small crowd clustered under the arch that led through to the dining rooms and restaurant; people just finishing up a leisurely breakfast, attracted by the noise, the schadenfreude of any accident scene.

This one was not going to be a fatality, I thought. Please God let this one not be a fatality.

"He has some medication," I said at one point to the woman EMT. She focused on me for the first time. "What is it?"

"I don't know," I said, and even I could hear the desperation in my voice. "He took it last night. From his pocket."

"Mr. Carter?" she said in that same strange loud voice. "Can you hear me?"

"Of course I can hear you, ma'am. You're yelling."

Glenn and I exchanged glances over their heads, a flash of amusement.

"What medications are you on, Mr. Carter?"

"I don't remember the name." He sounded irritated. I'd be irritated, too, if I were in pain and someone were yelling in my face like that.

"It's in his pocket," I said again.

"Thank you, I heard you." She raised her voice again. "Mr. Carter, I'm going to get the medication from your pocket now."

They'd snapped a plastic oxygen mask over his nose by then, and he seemed to be breathing better, but it was clear he was looking for something, and in a moment I realized it was me. He reached up and loosened it so he could speak. "Did you call these people, Miss Sydney?"

I nodded. "Yes, Howard," I said.

"Then that's something else we will need to discuss together." He let them take him out then, leaving the rest of us standing around watching the doorway through which they'd disappeared.

"What was that about?" asked Mike.

"Damned if I know," I said.

***

I'd seen Jordan in the fringes of the breakfast crowd, and as they started to dissipate I
walked over to her. "Hey. How're you feeling?"

"Okay. I guess." She managed a smile. She
was wearing jeans and a sweater with what
looked like several complicated necklaces. Jordan, I was learning, made whatever she was
currently wearing look like precisely what was
called for in the moment, with a dollop of cre-
ativity on top. I don't rock jeans like that; I
generally look as though I looked at what
clothing in my "clean" pile and grabbed whatever was on top.

Well, I *do* have to go to the laundromat to
wash my clothes. That often tends to limit my
choices somewhat.

Unaware of my sartorial comparisons, Jordan had her own agenda. "Have you heard anything about Reggie? How the investigation is
going?"

I frowned. There's something intrinsically
wrong about the wedding planner being the
go-to person for information about crime

investigations. "I was going to ask you the same thing," I said.

She shook her head. "I haven't heard anything," she said. "Who was that they just took out?"

Of course; she was particularly sensitive to gurneys right now, having last seen one with her wife's body on it. "A guest at the inn," I said.

"What happened to him?"

I shrugged. "I'm not sure. Maybe a heart attack. Maybe a panic attack." I'd heard they looked similar.

She hesitated. "What was his name?"

I looked at her curiously. "Howard Carter." All right, so wedding planners don't have confidentiality agreements with their clients. "Why?"

She didn't answer. She cleared her throat. "I'm expecting to—they said I need to go and formally identify Reggie. As a family member, I mean."

I shivered. That sounded like that last thing in the world anyone wanted to do. Of course it was the last thing in the world anyone wanted to do. "I'm so sorry," I said, the words inadequate. What else can you say?

Jordan said, abruptly, "Will you come with me?"

"Excuse me?" I was still dwelling on the sadness aspect of the whole thing.

"I have to go to the medical examiner's office," said Jordan. "They've already performed the autopsy. I have to identify her. Then we can start the red tape for getting her home." She took a deep breath. "I want her buried in the park. At Africville. I think that's what she'd want."

"Um…" I was trying to do sums in my head. The Cape Cod satellite medical examiner's office is in Sandwich, pretty much the opposite side of the Cape from Provincetown. Even in October, with less traffic, it would take well over an hour to get there. And well over an hour to get back. And I still had to sort my three o'clock wedding; the rain had, if anything, intensified. If they were still determined to be married outside, I was going to have to enlist help to put up the tent. In the rain. There was no way I could go to Sandwich.

Jordan was still talking. "They said I could take a taxi," she said. "I just don't feel comfortable doing that. Going alone, with some driver I don't know who will probably want to talk to me… And, plus—well, it's awkward to talk about—but that sounds very expensive…"

It was. She could get the bus for a fraction of the cost, but she'd have to make a connection in Hyannis and who knew what the bus routes were into Sandwich? Off the top of my head, I thought a taxi would probably be two hundred dollars.

Each way.

You'd think that one of the Staties could take pity on her and send her in a cruiser. But they were all apparently very busy with other important things. Like not solving this murder.

I took a deep breath. "We'll figure something out," I temporized. Maybe I could find someone to drive her to Sandwich. I could ask Glenn or Mike to call in one of the kids they had tending bar or working the front desk—*they* didn't make two hundred dollars an hour, and the inn has a couple of vehicles. I didn't have to actually get in the Little Green Car and drive her myself.

Though on the way back from Sandwich one could check in at Cape Cod Hospital in Hyannis, where the ambulance was taking Howard Carter even as we spoke. It seemed that if someone collapsed when talking to you, you could at least take an interest in their continued survival. Even if you didn't particularly like them.

I spared a fleeting thought for the fiancée, Lydia, but I expected that the hospital would take care of contacting her. They're actually very efficient, as I learned last June when I broke my arm. Painfully efficient, emphasis on the pain part.

In any case, the day was off to a very exciting start.

9

I left Jordan looking pensive and lost at the same time, shimmied behind the reception desk to my little cubbyhole, and started making calls.

Mike, first. Jordan might look lost and wistful and make one want to save her, but I also had a job to do. "This rain's not letting up," I said.

"Good observation."

"There's a wedding at three o'clock."

"So? No problem? Bring it inside."

"They won't." I went through an abbreviated version of the women's meeting and their determination to reenact it at the precise place and time.

"Cripes," said Mike. "Who remembers at what *time* they meet?"

"Women do," I assured him. I wondered, fleetingly, what had put that particular trait in our DNA, some survival skill left over from the days of living in caves, something that made us hyper-aware of the relationships that webbed our environments so we could know who to count on to help keep the wild out. Not that I'd picked up that particular gene; I actually think I'm the least observant person on the planet. To every rule, an exception. "Anyway, we're going to need the tent."

"Cripes," Mike said again. "You know how long it takes to set that up?"

"I do. That's why I'm telling you about it at nine-thirty."

He sighed and changed tack. "What happened to that guy this morning, Sydney? You were there, right? Your wedding guy—Howard Carter?"

"It may have been a heart attack," I said. I don't have much experience with heart attacks, though not as little as I'd like. "He's alive. They transported him."

"Yeah, I know. I'll give the hospital a call. It doesn't look good for us."

"Never mind the Race Point Inn, it doesn't look good for Howard, either," I said a little tartly. "Mike—I don't know if you saw him before that? There was something going on. He was waiting for me at reception when I came

in, just waiting to see me. He was very unhappy. In fact, he was... angry? Maybe? He
was as close to rude as a southern gentleman
probably allows himself to be."

"Hmm." Mike thought for a moment.
"You know what that was about?"

"Haven't a clue," I said. "Can you get my
tent set up?"

A long sigh. He was going to do it, he just
wanted me to know I'd owe him. In reality, the
wedding would be as perfect as possible, the
women would be joyous, and we were guaran-
teed they'd return to the inn every Women's
Week and would probably throw in an anni-
versary party or two as well. It was a dance we
did, Mike and me. "I guess we can manage."

I decided not to press my luck. I'd ask
Glenn about the ride to Sandwich. "Thanks,
Mike."

"Yeah, yeah," he growled and put down
the phone. I held mine in my hand for a moment, thinking. Some things are best done in
person.

I tracked Glenn down in his lair, a big
comfortable office where a photograph of
Barry, Glenn's longtime partner and my first
boss at the inn, took pride of place on the wall.
Glenn hadn't set out to own the Race Point: it

was Barry's, but when his partner was murdered, Glenn stepped up to the plate and had run it ever since. And he'd done a fabulous job, even I had to admit. We were year-round prosperous, a destination within a destination, and it wasn't *all* down to Adrienne the diva chef.

Glenn's office was another place where, once upon a time, there had been violence. I was starting to collect these spaces around town. Here, I'd almost lost Ali. I couldn't ever not think of it every time I walked in the door.

I was a little surprised to hear voices inside, and paused. A woman saying something, and some other sound—gurgling? I knocked and swung the door open and stood for a moment taking in the scene. Glenn sitting on the floor. Mirela sitting on one of his client chairs. And down with Glenn, on her stomach and chuckling with delight, Lily.

Mirela was calm. Mirela is always calm. "It is your godmother," she said to the baby. She was, meantime, doing something on her smartphone. "Here," she said to Glenn, passing it over to him. "Here she is with my mother."

He took the phone and checked out the photo. "She's simply gorgeous, Mirela," he said, and then to my horror pitched his voice up. "Aren't you, honey? Aren't you adorable?"

Next he was going to say, "totes adorbs." If I hadn't had other things on my mind, I'd have called him on it.

He noticed me, then. "Hey, Sydney."

"Glenn," I said. I was peering at Lily. While she was undeniably beginning to develop recognizable features, gorgeous wasn't a word to be bandied about lightly. Besides, all I could see was the back of her head.

Mirela said, "We came to see *you*, sunshine, but Uncle Glenn kidnapped us."

Uncle Glenn? "Um, great." I looked at the squirming child on the floor. "Is she old enough to be doing that?" Not that I know the first thing about children, but applesauce and crawling seemed a little precocious. She still looked a lot like a blob with limbs to me.

Besides, on the floor?

Mirela was watching me and I had the uncomfortable feeling she was reading my mind. Glenn said, "That's right. Lily's a star, aren't you? Aren't you, sweetheart?"

I cleared my throat. "Glenn, I have a favor to ask."

"See? That's what happens when you grow up," he told Lily. "You start being demanding." He looked up at me, a smile softening the words. "I can't remember the last time I played on the floor," he said.

I had no idea what to say to that. I said, "I have no idea what to say to that. Can you do something for me?"

He pulled himself with some effort into a sitting position. Lily immediately squawked. He lifted her as though she weighed nothing—to be fair, next to his bulk, she did in fact weigh nothing—and nestled her on his lap. "What can I do for you?"

Mirela said, "And here is the portrait I am working on." She handed the phone back across to Glenn.

"Nice," he said. "What can I do for you, Sydney?"

I cleared my throat. "Jordan Bellefort is supposed to go to the medical examiner's office to formally identify her wife's body," I said. "I'd like to offer her a ride, but I have a three o'clock wedding."

"I remember. You moved that inside, right?" He was juggling Lily up and down, and she was making that gurgling noise again.

"No. They won't do it. Mike's getting the tent set up."

"It'll be cold," Glenn said, frowning. "Rain and wind. Are they sure?"

Would I be here if they weren't? "They're sure," I said. "But the point is, I have to be here. To—coordinate things. And I'm thinking it would be nice if we could help Jordan out. Get her a ride to Sandwich."

"I don't know," said Glenn. "That seems a little above and—"

Mirela interrupted. "I will drive her," she said.

We both gaped at her. Mirela owns a car—she bought one last spring when she came back from Bulgaria with her niece in tow—but, being Mirela, she didn't buy the standard new-mommy SUV. She bought a 1962 Ferrari 250 GTE, and the only reason she didn't get an Alfa Romeo Spider was that someone told her she had to put Lily in the back seat—hence the need for a back seat.

She also didn't drive it much. She had an indoor garage space and most of the time she bicycled around town—like the rest of us—and ignored the car. I'd only ever been in it twice since she bought it. Glenn hadn't ever—I seriously doubted he'd fit.

"Are you sure?" I asked. "I mean, it's—"

"I know what it is, sunshine," she said calmly. "Lily and I will take her to Sandwich. She cannot go and identify the body of her love on her own."

I wasn't sure that identifying the body of your love with a baby looking on was going to be much of an improvement, but what do I know?

"Well, there you are," said Glenn to me, in an *everybody-happy-now?* kind of voice.

"Okay," I said cautiously. I was waiting for the catch. I had no idea why Mirela would offer. It's not that she isn't altruistic, just that she lives in her own inner artsy world and doesn't always pay attention to what's going on around her. Maybe Lily was mellowing her.

Or maybe she had something up her sleeve. With Mirela, you never knew.

***

There was a problem with the chocolates.

Philip had ventured out from his cavernous kitchens to deliver the bad news: the evening wedding was supposed to have chocolates delivered from Switzerland—one of the brides was Swiss—to have one at each place in the dining room. "So what's the problem?" I asked.

"The problem is, no chocolates, doll," said Philip. "They were supposed to be here last night. I called this morning. The *pralinés émotion*," he said, getting the accent right as far as I could tell, "left Favarger, in Geneva, day before yesterday as planned. But they've been held up in Customs."

"Is that usual?"

He shrugged. "A couple of years ago I had a boyfriend ordered them for me for my birthday," he said. "They were right on time."

I blew out a sigh. "And what's so special about them?"

He was ready for me. He whipped out a piece of paper. "That would be the incomparable flavor of hazelnuts or almonds delicately caramelized in a copper cauldron, the extreme creaminess of pralines, ground so finely in a stone grinder, the crispiness of a feuilletine, the freshness of a lemony note, the pleasure of a great Swiss chocolate... The emotion of authentic, intense, sensual and sophisticated flavors," he said.

"Well, then." So glad I asked. Not much you could respond to that, was there? It didn't really matter whether they had sensual and sophisticated flavors or tasted like a Hershey's bar, they were clearly not going to be on my table by seven. "Chequessett," I decided.

"Are they open?" Starting in October, we always wonder. The town shuts down slowly, one venue at a time.

"They make chocolate year-round," I said. The fact is, they specialize in chocolate bars— amazing chocolate bars with local names like Wellfleet Sea Salt and Nantucket Nib Crunch and Aquinnah Almond & Cherry and Moonlight Mooncusser—but I had a feeling that a quick call could deliver something splendid to put next to the plates. It had to be good: Adrienne the diva chef was overseeing the wedding. "Call Katie Reed," I said. "Explain the problem, see what she suggests."

"And *you'll* tell the brides, doll?"

I smiled. "Yeah, Philip, I'll tell the brides. I get to do the dangerous stuff; that's why they pay me the medium bucks."

Maybe he could order an extra bit of chocolate for me, I thought, turning away. There aren't too many problems which the immediate application of chocolate won't help, if not actually fix.

My day hadn't really actually started yet and I'd packed one client off to the hospital, arranged for another to get taken to the morgue, and solved the Great Chocolate Dilemma.

Some days are definitely more exciting than others.

10

I tracked Jordan down in the lounge and told her about the change in plans. "It's ridiculous for you to go alone. It's a traumatic moment, a traumatic event. It will help to have someone with you. My friend Mirela's gone home to take care of a few things, but she'll be back to drive you."

"You're sure you can't come? Only, I know you, I feel comfortable with you…" What she sounded was scared. Impulsively, I reached over and took her hand. "Listen, Jordan, I can't tell you that everything's going to be all right, because I have no idea if it's true or not. And I know damned well that nothing's all right, right now. But you're not alone here. You have friends."

She nodded. "Thank you," she said. "I think I'm going to organize my research while I wait. See what I can get done while I'm still here. I'm obviously not staying the full two weeks, not now."

Grief takes different people in different ways. Some sit around staring into space. I remember when my aunt died, I came upon my uncle—they'd been married for over forty years—coming down from the attic, a lamp in hand. "Been meaning to rewire this thing forever," he said. (Of course, this was the same uncle who a week later was caught staring at a can of Campbell's soup. "You know what to do with this?" he asked me.)

Jordan fell into the keep-busy category. "We have a library on the second floor," I told her. "You might want to work there. There's a big table and some fairly good lighting." She was going to need it, on a gray day like today. "Mirela will come and get you when she's ready to leave for Sandwich."

Thus reminded of various coping methods, I called Thea to see how hers was coming along. I left a message—she was no doubt seeing a patient at the Outer Cape Heath Center—and then looked around, a little wildly, for my list.

I love lists. I truly do. How else can you feel totally organized and go in for a little self-flagellation (when you don't check every item off, and who ever checks every item off?) at the same time? It's a terrific two-fer. When you can't find the list, though, all bets are off: you're left wallowing in a sea of confusion. And even more guilt, because you lost the thing.

I am Catholic. I am also my mother's daughter. Guilt, you might say, is *my* spécialité de la maison. When I'm not feeling anxious, I'm feeling guilty. Other people have stronger coping skills and better comfort zones. My comfort zone is a beach in Antigua. Lacking that, anxiety and guilt will have to do.

My phone vibrated: a text from Ali. Good. I could use a little grounding right now. *Cara, heading out of town for a few days.*

Nope: this wasn't good. My stomach immediately developed a bad case of butterflies. Deliberately misunderstanding, I texted back, *Somewhere fun I hope.*

He was short on time, and probably on patience. *Work.*

Well, I *knew* that. *How long? Can you talk on phone?* Of course he couldn't, he would have called if he could call.

Not now. Hope to be back by the weekend. Talk then. Love you.

Hell. I'd insulted a client into the hospital, was probably going to be stuck babysitting a six-month-old while Mirela took Jordan to Sandwich, had a wedding in the rain, needed to solve the Case of the Disappearing Chocolates, and now my own support system had vanished, possibly to do something unspeakably dangerous in some far-off place whose location I'd never learn. Ibsen had better not be cranky tonight, that was all I could say. What else could possibly go wrong?

Here's a tip: never say things like that. You're just tempting the gods.

I tempted them even more by calling Julie Agassi. "Sydney Riley," she answered. "Just on time. I thought it must be—oh, what, a whole ten hours since you asked me if there was any progress on the case."

"More like twelve," I said encouragingly. "Is there?"

"And I should tell you, why?" But there was a lightness about Julie that was as refreshing as it was unfamiliar. Something had changed. For one thing, she didn't seem to want to take my head off every time I asked her anything.

"Because you love me so?"

She made a sound like "hunh."

"And because I've been not entirely un-helpful in solving a mystery or two around the place," I added.

"They're called homicides, Sydney, not mysteries. You've been reading too much Agatha Christie again."

"You say potato, I say mystery. So what do you have?"

She sighed. "You'll be the death of me," she predicted. But there was that same lightness in her voice. I wondered if she'd met someone. I was definitely going to have to follow up on that. I'd put it on my list, if I ever found the list.

"And?"

"And we've tracked the bartender down."

"Ah," I said in satisfaction. Hadn't I kept pointing that out? The Case of the Disappearing Bartender. More Nancy Drew than Agatha Christie, I decided. "Where is he? Did he do it?"

"He's here," she said, and there was no mistaking what was in her voice now: satisfaction. "I'm sure later today the Staties will come and have a chat with him, but they might be delayed, there's something going on in Hyannis, some big drug bust."

"So for now he's yours."

"So for now he's mine," she agreed. "Catch and release. We know where he lives, we can always get him back, and I don't want them accusing me of holding him when they're not here. I'm not treading on their toes any more than I have to."

I was thinking. This could be worth braving the rain for. "I don't suppose I could come by and…"

"No," she snapped, momentarily back to the Julie Agassi I knew and loved. "No, you could not." Then the softening again. "But I can tell you he's involved."

"How? Who is he?"

"He's a local. Does gigs all over town in the season—and I know you're a barfly, but you probably haven't noticed him, he's only recently graduated to mixing cocktails. Before this he's been a bar back."

Bar back. The most grueling job of all. Lugging cases of liquid up from the cellar, down from the attic, from wherever the restaurant or bar stored it (and you could be sure it wouldn't be in a convenient place, convenient real estate is at a premium in those establishments), constantly in motion, constantly lifting. You get great muscles. You also get a great attitude. I'd feel murderous after a shift as a bar back.

Who am I kidding? I wouldn't last ten *minutes* as a bar back.

"In fact," Julie was saying, "This was his début, and he only got it because the woman who was supposed to be bartending for the Dinner got sick. Someone grabbed him a manual on mixing cocktails and he got promoted on the spot.

"That's not helpful," I complained. "If he was the one who killed her, he'd have had to be sure he was going to be in the right spot at the right time. Last-minute changes aren't good for plans."

"They are when you engineer them," said Julie. "We're pretty sure the original bartender—you know her, Patty Simons—was poisoned. Not enough to kill her, enough to incapacitate her."

The plot was thickening. "So he killed Reggie? Is that what you're thinking?"

"I'm not thinking anything yet," she said. "Evidence, then hypotheses. If you really want to be an amateur detective, you need to memorize that. Don't get ahead of yourself."

I wasn't at all sure I actually wanted to be an amateur detective, not if you phrased it like that, though I suppose it was descriptive enough. Not the time to ask for lessons. "What do you have on him? And what's his name, anyway?"

"Jed Paltrow."

"I never heard of him," I said.

An exaggerated sigh. "I think that's what I've been trying to tell you," said Julie. "You know, Sydney, three thousand people live in P'town. Try as you might, you can't know every single one of them."

Who was she thinking I was? The town gossip? I don't hang out in the right bars for that. "Where does he live? Who's he friends with?" Provincetown as a community encompasses a tremendous number of sub-communities, some based on friendship, others on sexual preference, gender identification, history, family, religion, common interests... the list goes on.

It's always fascinated me that a place like this can be seen almost in layers, the layers of what is really here—and then, totally separately, of what we *perceive* to be here. And that everybody perceives something different.

I walk down Commercial Street, and I see—okay, mostly, I see food and drink, I won't lie, my eye picks out restaurants I like.

174

And I see people, people I know, people I know I should know but can't quite place, people I just recognize in a general way, people I dismiss as visitors who aren't staying at the Race Point Inn because I don't know them at all.

Ali walks down Commercial Street with me and he sees what's in people's eyes—and in their hands; he's clocked a shoplifter before. Ali's a cop, even when he's not working.

Philip, the sous-chef from the restaurant, walks down Commercial Street and—because he has a drag act of his own—he notices men he knows to also be performers, he notices the makeup and hairdressing places, he can go by the Provincetown Florist/Hair by the Sea and tell you precisely how many tiaras are in the window after merely a cursory glance.

Mirela walks down Commercial Street and sees the galleries, who's moved a different painting into the window, what artist created the painting, and whether it's up to her standard. She can do that in a flash.

Glenn walks down Commercial Street and unerringly picks out the bears, knows who's new, who's been coming to the Bear Week and Out of Hibernation celebrations since they started, who's been dating whom, who got his heart broken.

I could do on and on. We all have our own points of reference, we all have things we see and other things to which we're totally blind. And the things we notice on Commercial Street? They're the things that are important to us. It's important for me to focus on people (potential clients) and restaurants (potential competition, though mostly it's not that, it's just I like to eat out). It's important for Ali to always be aware of his surroundings from a safety point of view, see what nefarious activities might be going on. It's important that Mirela keep her eye on the pulse of the artistic community. It's important that Glenn and Philip connect with their peeps. And so on.

The same goes for entertainment. A smattering of glitter in a doorway says nothing to me, but it speaks volumes to the people who attended the party the night before that left that kind of glitter behind. I'm not on top of what people buy in the leather shops—or what they do with their purchases afterward—but I know there are sly looks exchanged when people arrive at Club Purgatory for Leather Night. It doesn't mean we live in different places, we just experience different layers of the same

space. And that's only dealing with the present—don't get me started on the past, on the
ghosts who share this space with us.

But it does really mean that we're, all of us,
wandering around in totally unrelated worlds
even as we walk down the same street.

I've lived and worked in P'town for a lot
of years, so while I don't belong to all the various communities that make up our one big
reasonably happy family, I can at least identify
many of them. Knowing who this Jed person
hangs out with would tell me a lot about who
he was, what he was into, who might know
something about him, where he might be
found. In P'town, for better or for worse,
community is everything.

Now I said to Julie, "What do you know
about this guy? And why is he still in town?"

"He's kind of a newbie," she said, not answering the question directly, following her
own thoughts instead. "Arrived here at the
start of the season, back in May."

"From where?"

"I'm looking." A moment as she riffled
through her notebook. "Newport News, Virginia," she said. "Must've been a navy brat. It's
all Navy and Coast Guard around there."

I didn't ask how she knew; Julie moves in mysterious ways.

"Like I said, been working bar backs all summer. Too much competition for the main stage." One of the highest-paying summer jobs in Provincetown is bartending, particularly if you're an attractive young man. Still, something had kept this Jed character behind the scenes, you don't spend five months behind the scenes and never get a chance to show your mad bartending skills up front unless there's a problem.

"What was wrong with him?" I asked. "That's got to be a clue."

"Believe it or not, Riley"—she only ever calls me Riley when she's getting exasperated—"we're actually on that. Along with a few other questions they teach us to ask at the police academy."

"Okay, point taken." Her good will couldn't go on forever.

"Before I forget it," Julie said, "your guy Howard Carter? Got transported to Cape Cod Hospital an hour ago?"

I felt my stomach lurch. *Don't die, Howard.* "Yeah?"

"He's on his way back. False alarm. Panic attack. Told to take it easy. Told to get a hobby. Thought you'd want to know."

I let my breath out; I didn't know I'd been holding it. "Thanks, Julie." A thought occurred. "How's he getting back?" The EMTs only take you one way when they transport; you're on your own after that.

"He has money, your guy. Hired a private car and driver. Have to go."

I clicked off, relief washing over me. I was still going to have to deal with whatever Howard's problem with me was, but I'd rather it that way than scheduling a funeral.

I stopped in the lounge and picked up a tray with coffee and the few remaining pastries—I wasn't exaggerating when I say Angus' work sells out fast—and headed up to the library. The memory of ghosts on Commercial Street had gotten me thinking.

Maybe Jordan would tell me more about her story.

11

Books and papers covered every inch of the library table. Jordan had a laptop open and was typing into it when I came in. "Knock-knock. Thought you could use a break."

She looked up and smiled. "That sounds good," she said. "I keep thinking that doing the work will keep my mind off Reggie, but…"

"It's hard," I agreed. "Every thought leads back somehow." At least that was my experience.

"Exactly." She made room for the tray on the table. "Those look really good."

I beamed at her. Her appetite returning had to be a good sign, right? "Angus is a genius," I said. "Help yourself."

I sat down across from her and sipped the coffee. The Race Point is secretive about its roasters. For good reason. "I was just thinking about all the layers of history we have in this town," I went on. "You know, not just people we've known who've died, but going way back... who lived here during the bohemian days, which old fishermen came stumbling out of the Old Colony, even going back to the Wampanoag."

"The who?" She looked startled.

"The tribes that lived here before the Europeans arrived," I said. "That was the general name. There were other tribes under that umbrella—the Pamet in Truro, the Mashpee up-Cape, the Aquinnah on the Vineyard, but Wampanoag's the generic name for them all. It means People of the First Light."

"That's really interesting," Jordan said. "Where I come from, in Nova Scotia, the First Nations tribe was called Children of Light. Well, we're all on the east coast, aren't we." She was unspiraling a sticky pastry. "Are they all dead?" she asked suddenly.

"The Wampanoag?" I was startled. "Good lord, no. There's a reservation on-Cape and another on the mainland somewhere—Taunton, maybe?" She was still eating, so I kept talking. "They have the only language that ever completely died out and was rediscovered and reintroduced. Some tribal members on the

Vineyard partnered with some linguistics geek at MIT and they actually brought the language back." I'm a star at my friend Michelle Crone's team trivia nights.

But I didn't want to talk about the Wampanoag. "So, anyway, the ghosts," I said. "I wondered—"

"Who else?" Jordan interrupted.

"Who else?"

"What other ghosts are in town? For sure, the aboriginal people, that's a given, they must haunt the whole continent." She shrugged. "In Nova Scotia, it's similar, there are a lot of First Nations tribes, but most of them are part of the Mi'kmaq nation." She smiled, suddenly, vividly.

"What?" I asked, smiling too. It was infectious, Jordan's smile.

"I just like their legends," she said. "They have this hero-god called Glooscap."

"Great name," I commented.

"Right? And there's a story about how the tides at the Bay of Fundy started— Mi'kmaq legend says that Fundy's great tide was created when Glooscap decided he wanted to take a bath. He commanded Beaver to build a dam at the mouth of the bay to trap the water for his bath. But that angered Whale, and he

183

demanded to know what had stopped the flow of the water. So Glooscap, not wanting to annoy Whale, instructed Beaver to break the dam, but Whale was too impatient. He began to break away at the dam with his tail and these great movements set Fundy's waters in motion." The smile widened. "To this very day the waters of the bay continue to sway back and forth."

That was all fascinating, but I wanted to move up a few centuries. "Anyway, the ghosts," I said.

"There are plenty of them," said Jordan. She finished her pastry.

"I was more interested in yours," I said. "What've you found out about Callie? Or Sarah? Do you know for sure they were brought here, to the inn?"

She was looking at me. "Do you think she's a ghost? Sarah?"

Did I think she was a ghost? Did I have any idea? "I don't know," I said, a little helplessly. "I only ever have had one experience with—that sort of thing. And it wasn't here."

"Really?" She put her coffee cup down. "Will you tell me about it?" I hesitated, and Jordan reached across the table to put her hand on my arm. "Please. I'm trying so hard to—stay in my head, you know? As opposed to my heart? I'd love to hear your story."

I took a deep breath. The thing was, I wasn't sure myself how I felt about what I'd experienced; I talk lightly of ghosts, of memories, but I'm fitting them slowly into my worldview.

"Okay. I was in college, in Boston—well, Cambridge—and one summer I took a job up on the New Hampshire-Vermont border, house sitting this big estate that was right up against the Connecticut River. Big old mansion, years and years of history. The woman who lived there, the caretaker, had fallen in love with some guy out in Colorado and wanted to spend the summer with him. It was easy enough, just staying there and making sure nothing fell apart."

"It sounds ideal," Jordan said.

I shrugged. "I suppose so. Anyway, when we did the handover, Meri—that was the caretaker—said the house was haunted. She said the owner before the present absentee owner was an older man who had married a much younger woman he'd fallen completely for. She wanted to write a cookbook, so he had the kitchen totally remodeled for her. There were silver dollars sunk into the floor, I remember.

And she'd barely begun when she was killed. Some sort of accident, I don't remember the details."

Jordan picked up another pastry and began unspiraling it. "Go on," she said.

"Her husband was inconsolable." (was that even a word?) "He ended up going into his study—it was beautiful, with floor-to-ceiling bookcases and views off across the river— and shutting himself in, and dying. Meri thought he was the ghost."

"You didn't?"

"My dog—it was actually the one time in my life I had a dog—couldn't be forced to enter that room, so she felt something. I never did. And besides, I figured, if he were the ghost, he wouldn't be unhappy, after all, I was there to take good care of his house. Good care of that splendid kitchen."

"So what happened?"

I sighed. I never know how to tell this. "I took a job," I said. "Luncheon prep cook at a restaurant across the river, over in Windsor. I was bored just hanging out. I slept in one of the upstairs rooms, it looked out over the water on one side, and there was a glassed-in corridor on the other." Probably, I had concluded, it had once been a balcony of sorts.

"So I'd close the door at night and turn out the lights and hope to sleep."

"Hope to sleep?" Jordan arched an elegant eyebrow.

"Didn't happen much," I confessed. "Muffin—that was my dog, and no, I didn't name her—slept with me, and she'd wake me up during the night. Not intentionally. She'd be growling. I'd snap on the light and see she was tracking something moving across the room, her fur all bristling, her lips snarling. And of course I couldn't see a thing. After that happened, I slept with the light on. Didn't make a difference, but it made me feel better."

"So, go on, there's more, I can feel it."

"It was all the history around there, you know?" I said. I'd long ago contextualized my experiences. "It was another art colony, like P'town, once upon a time. During the Gilded Age, there were all these mansions strung up and down the river, and everybody took the train up from Boston and New York. Augustus Saint-Gaudens, the sculptor, had a place there; and Maxfield Parrish, too. Isadora Duncan came, and Ethyl Barrymore, the writer Percy MacKaye, Norman Hapgood... all these really illustrious people. And madder than hatters, all of them. Lots of drinks and drugs, wild parties. *Legendarily* wild parties."

"So what happened?"

I sighed. "So what happened was I had to get up early for the lunch prep, and I'd generally fall asleep okay, but then sometime around midnight, it would start."

She leaned forward. "What would start?"

This wasn't easy to tell. "I'd wake up and you would swear—I'd swear—there was a party going on, the other side of my door, out in the corridor. Music, and laughter, and people's voices. Sometimes a clinking glass." I took a deep breath. "I'd get up and open the door and look, and of course nothing was there, it was just a dusty old corridor with moonlight shining in on nothing. But the moment I'd close the door and get back in bed, it started again."

Jordan frowned. "Hmm," she said, then looked up with a smile. "Sure you weren't taking any of those drugs, yourself?" she asked.

I laughed. "It sounds like it," I admitted.

"So what happened?" she asked again.

This was perhaps the most embarrassing part. "This was in northern New Hampshire, you see, and my parents lived—well, they still do—in New Hampshire. So on a day off I drove down to see them for Sunday lunch. I didn't really mean to tell them, but it came out." And as soon as the words were out of my mouth I'd stopped, horrified. My family is Catholic. My mother is of the rabid variety, who manages to get to Mass two or three times a week, and thinks anyone who doesn't is a wuss. I could only imagine what she'd say. Ghosts? Go to confession. Tell Father your sins of imagination.

I looked at Jordan. I still couldn't quite believe what my mother had said. Pouring gravy delicately onto her stuffing, not even looking up at me, she said, "Well, Sydney, have you tried asking them to be quiet?"

Jordan laughed. "That's perfect!"

"It's not only perfect," I said ruefully, "it worked. That night I opened the door and said I had to be at work the next morning and they were keeping me awake. I spoke to an empty corridor. And there was no more noise that night, and anytime they bothered me again, I just asked them to stop."

"Considerate ghosts!"

"Yeah, they were." I didn't tell her about the rest, the reading of the local history, the fact of part of the estate was built over an

Abnaki burial ground. Muffin wouldn't go there, either—and after a while, neither did I.

"So those are your ghost stories," said Jordan.

I nodded. "My only one. Your turn."

She smiled, but her eyes were distant. "There are too many," she said. "There isn't anyone who isn't haunted, at the end of the day."

I had a feeling she wasn't talking about ghost stories anymore. "Tell me about Callie and Sarah," I said, because that seemed to please her, talking about her research. "How did you track down the plantation?"

Jordan laughed. "Oh, that was the easy part. It was there in her diary. She wasn't writing when she was living in Virginia, you know, that would have been too dangerous. But she remembered it all. Slaves had to develop peculiar ways of memorizing things, of communicating. They used to sing songs that had literal meanings, sure, but that had coded meanings inside them, too, eh? Secret meanings."

"Like what?"

She started to sing, instead of answering, that rich textured voice that spoke of smoke and fire. *Swing low, sweet chariot, coming for to carry me home. Swing low, sweet chariot, coming for the carry me home.* She looked at me. "Could be God," she said. "Could be the Underground Railroad. Carry me home? Could be heaven, could be freedom." She hummed for a moment, then the words followed. *I looked over Jordan, and what did I see? A band of angels coming after me… If you get there before I do, tell all my friends I'm coming after you.*

"Translation?" I asked.

"Mississippi or Ohio rivers for sure," she said. "The band of angels? That's the conductors. If you get there first, if I have escaped friends or family, tell them about my escape plan."

"Whew." We sat for a moment in silence, and then she began to hum again. No words, just that lilting music, and I could imagine the messages, wafting on the air, carried on the wind, plans and meetings and travel arrangements. "I was named for that river," said Jordan, quietly. "My family was always aware of where we came from."

"And the plantation?" I asked. "What became of it?"

"Talk about ghosts!" she said. "It's a historic site now. Tourists pay their fees and walk through and comment on how beautiful the house is and ask stupid questions."

"I can imagine."

She shook her head. "You really can't, Sydney," she said. "The things they ask—they're not just ignorant, they're demeaning. Like, what did the house slaves have to complain about, they got to work in such a pretty place?" She swallowed. "It's worth mentioning, the bulk of wanted ads placed in newspapers for fugitive slaves are for house servants, not field workers. Apparently whatever slavery was like in the big house, people were willing to risk their lives to get away from it."

"Like Callie and Sarah," I said softly. I wondered what Callie had done, besides read to the blind member of the family. I looked at her speculatively. "It sounds like you know this place," I said. "Are you sure you've never been there?"

She shook her head. "I've talked to people who have," she said. "Just research. Funny, though—Reggie always talked about going. I think she would have been even more interested in going to Virginia than she was in coming to Massachusetts. She felt really deeply for our people." She shrugged. "I'm interested in finding out, sure. But I think I know what I need to know. Provincetown? This was a way for me to draw a line under it all. After this, I think I'm going to just focus on my music."

"I'm sorry Reggie didn't have the opportunity. You must regret that."

"No." She must have realized how abrupt she'd sounded, because she added, "I don't think she could bear the tourists. If they're like the ones who come to Africville, they're mostly white. It might be their Downton Abbey," she said and shrugged. "It's our American Horror Story."

I didn't say anything. The truth was, I didn't know what to say. What had started as a lighthearted discussion had gone someplace else, someplace darker, someplace scarier. Talking about it, really talking about it, was uncomfortable as hell. Did I have any slave owners in *my* family tree?

Probably.

For a short, sharp moment I wondered if this were one of the reasons Ali did what he did. He couldn't change the system, but he could rescue people who were being enslaved by it. Somewhere in this country, perhaps closer than I thought (*"much* closer than you think," Ali said to me once), someone like Callie or Sarah was scrubbing floors in a mansion or reading to someone's children or having sex they didn't want to have. Some were Black, some were Asian, some were Latinx, some were white. What they had in common was that their bodies belonged to someone else.

Jordan looked at me. "It makes you uncomfortable," she said.

I nodded.

"At least you're honest about it," she said. "People come to Africville and they say, oh, what poor conditions, and wasn't it better before they escaped, when they lived in those big southern plantations? Maybe slavery wasn't that bad." She shrugged. "Me, I think it's all about feelings of guilt for the past." She looked at me. "You don't want your ancestors to have done bad things because you don't want to think of yourself as a bad person." She sighed. "Anyway, blame and guilt aren't really the point of telling the histories of enslaved people. The point is to honor people whose stories haven't been told. And, besides, they're not wrong about Africville. The poverty was appalling."

"But it was better to be free," I said. I didn't know if it was a statement or a question.

"Poverty's poverty," said Jordan. "I don't think they knew what to expect. Callie and

Sarah. What does freedom look like, for some-one who's never known freedom before?"

It looks, I thought, like the bottom of a smelly fishing-boat on a cold wild Atlantic night. Probably not what anyone had imag-ined.

My phone was vibrating, and I picked it up. "Mirela," I said.

"Yes, sunshine, I am here, and where are you?"

I glanced across at Jordan. "In the library," I said. It had felt like a schoolroom.

"You are reading books?" She seemed to find that amusing. "I have the car outside, and Lily in it, and Mike is looking after her but he looks nervous."

"Oh, so it's Uncle Glenn, but not Uncle Mike?"

"Sunshine," she said severely "Not every-one understands about babies."

You're telling me. "I'll tell Jordan you're ready to go," I said and disconnected.

She wouldn't look at me. "Time to see Reggie," she said.

I swallowed and nodded. "Jordan, I'm so sorry."

She stood up, started moving papers around the table a little blindly. I realized she was crying. "Just leave it all," I said. "I'll lock the door; no one will disturb it."

She nodded, her head still down, still not speaking. I opened the door for her. "I can stop by your room, get your coat for you." She was going to need it; the rain was coming down in sheets. Welcome to the seashore.

"It's all right," said Jordan, dashing tears away with the back of her hand. "I'll do it. I'll see you here later?"

I touched her shoulder. "Good luck."

She nodded and headed down the hallway, only once stumbling against the wall. I couldn't bear to think what she must be feeling.

It took me a few minutes to find the key to the library door. I pulled it shut, and as I did, I could smell a wave of perfume, sweet, strong. Neither Jordan nor I had been wearing it.

I wondered if Sarah might still be hanging around, after all.

12

I remember I once told Ali he could be himself and live his life however he liked. We hadn't been talking about racism or xenophobia, not directly; I think the conversation up until then had been about law enforcement, if I'm remembering correctly. And he gave me a quizzical smile—Ali does quizzical smiles well—and said, "I can understand how you'd see it that way."

At the time I thought he was being ever-so-slightly patronizing, the way some people say, "I'm sorry you feel that way," when they're really not, when they don't want to own responsibility. But more and more since then, I've recalled the wistfulness in what he said, the acknowledgment that we really do only see what our experience and our beliefs allow us— maybe even lead us—to see.

***

I was thinking that all the orchestration around Reggie's murder couldn't have been carried out by one person. I had a feeling that Julie (and the state police, though I was tending to dismiss them for no reason other than turf resentment) was going to come to the same conclusion. Jed the first-time-because-someone-was-poisoned bartender was undoubtedly part of the plot, but even without talking to him myself, I wasn't getting the cunning criminal mastermind vibe. No one spends that much time lugging cartons of bottles up and down stairs in the heat of summer if they have other career alternatives.

No offense to bar backs, of course.

Julie told me once that the question to ask about any crime, but especially about murder, was this: what changed in the soon-to-be-criminal's life that made it necessary to do this murder, at this time, in this place? Unless someone's a professional assassin or part of a crime family, murder isn't in general anybody's first strategy of choice. The stakes are high: too many things can go wrong, and the consequences if apprehended are severe. So something changed. If you can find out what that was, Julie said, then you're on the right track to figure out who acted on those changed circumstances.

In Reggie's case, the most obvious immediate change was that she was in the United States.

Julie's the expert, of course, but I've been involved in enough of these situations that I've added my own question: why Provincetown?

It's not a ridiculous thing to ask. We really *are* at land's end. We're a former fishing village at the end of a sandbar that's a resort in the summer and nothing but a long stretch of loneliness in the winter. People come here for a lot of reasons: for fun and pleasure, to lose themselves, sometimes even to find themselves. They come here to get married or to break up. They come here to fall in love or to write the Great American Novel or to paint the light on the water. What they don't do is come here haphazardly.

Occasionally, they come here for murder. And every time that's happened, there's been a reason they came here, specifically to P'town, to do it.

So assuming someone already wanted to kill Reggie, why did they have to do it here?

What was keeping them from doing it in Halifax?

And what I kept coming back to was Jordan's project. Jordan was the one who had to be in Provincetown.

What was it about research into the Underground Railroad that had proven so deadly?

***

Howard Carter arrived back at the Race Point Inn with minimal fanfare. His driver walked him to the door, holding an umbrella over his head, and he seemed, if anything, somewhat sheepish behind his dark glasses. At least that was the vibe I was getting off him. He was tipping his hat to anyone who looked his way in the lobby, and he was leaning on a cane he hadn't been carrying before.

I was in my cubbyhole behind the reception desk and probably could have lurked there indefinitely, but, as I like to say (and probably do, ad infinitum, ad nauseam), that's why they pay me the medium bucks. "Mr. Carter! How are you feeling?"

"Howard," he reminded me. "And I owe you a debt of gratitude, Miss Sydney, I surely do. Scared the bejeezus out of me, what happened this morning."

I didn't want to say how scared I'd been as well. Cool as a cucumber, that's Sydney Riley. "I'm glad it wasn't serious," I said instead.

He leaned an elbow on the reception counter. "Do you know what that Yankee doctor said to me? He says I'm to lower my stress. That's what he told me. Lower my stress. I told him, all right then, once I've finished what I'm here for, I'm taking a long vacation. Yes, siree, that's what I'm going to be doing. I've thought about it all the way back, in the car. A vacation is just what the doctor ordered." He winked at me. "Literally, in my case!"

"That sounds nice," I said. "With Lydia? Where do you plan to go?" And where do your wedding plans fit in?

"Lydia?" He seemed momentarily disconcerted. "Ah, yes, of course, my lovely fiancée. We'll have to see if she can take the time off from work. Don't like to push her too much. A busy lady. Always going to New York City, always off in meetings." He smiled. "Maybe this'll get her to slow down a little, what do you think, Miss Sydney?"

I smiled back at him. "That would probably be good for both of you. And it's just

Sydney, Howard, really." I hesitated. "Howard—I just want to make sure everything's okay. You seemed angry about something this morning. I wouldn't like to think that something I did led to your—attack."

He looked startled. "Did I?"

Yeah, you did. "It doesn't matter," I said, mentally kicking myself for bringing it up. I'd only done it to assuage my own guilt, because I was obsessing on it, and here he had doctors telling him to lower his stress. "Would you like to go to your suite and rest? I can have something sent up to you."

"Iced tea?"

In October? "Of course," I said smoothly.

"Not that anyone north of the Mason-Dixon Line's ever made a decent glass of iced tea in their life, but you may surprise me, young lady. And it's true that I'm a mite tired. All this rushing around, it can't be good for the constitution."

I smiled; I couldn't help it. "I'd expect not," I said. "And we'll see how the inn's iced tea measures up."

He tipped his hat to me and headed toward the elevator. I called room service and ordered iced tea with sugar and lemon on the side, and any fruit they had lying around so he'd have something healthy to snack on, and told them to deliver it to the Harry Kemp suite.

I'd decided there was something else I wanted to do.

Here's the truth about me: I'm nosy. I prefer to call it insatiable intellectual curiosity, but let's be honest here, that's just another term for nosiness.

My case is well documented. Ask anyone: my boyfriend, my bosses, my friends, my police contacts. It's not an attractive trait, though it does explain why I'm so eager to play Nancy Drew anytime anything untoward happens in P'town.

And it's part and parcel of my profession. I know I make them look easy, thank you very much, but weddings are actually tricky things—check with anyone who's ever had a hand in organizing one—and one of the reasons I stay on top of everything that can go wrong is that I ask nosy questions. Is the groom's first wife going to show up out of the blue and embarrass everybody? Do you think that veil's going to withstand Cape Cod winds? Is the best man likely to get smashed before he even makes the wedding toast?

It's not like there was anything else urgently requiring my attention, or so I told myself. Mike and his minions were out in the rain and wind, wearing oilskins and struggling to put up the tent and probably swearing a blue streak. Separate cases of champagne for the two weddings *du jour* were cooling in their separate spaces in the wine cellar (Veuve Cliquot for one, Dom Pérignon for the other).

Mirela was driving Jordan west on Route Six, certainly in Eastham by now, possibly all the way onto Suicide Alley, the stretch of road where there's only one lane going in either direction and headlight use is mandated.

Both officiants had already texted me that everything was ready from their points of view. The three o'clock couple was up-Cape somewhere picking up their rings, and the evening couple was at Town Hall picking up their marriage license. Guests were hanging out everywhere there was a place to hang out.

I went upstairs to lock the library. I told myself that was my intention, and even as I did I was lying to myself. I'll lock the library, I told myself virtuously, then go and make some calls. Wedding planners are forever making calls.

I opened the door, just to make sure the light was turned off, mind you—our library's an interior room, so no light from any window doth break—and some voice inside me said, *maybe just tidy the papers a little. Jordan doesn't want to come back to this mess. Not when she's just been identifying Reggie's body.*

If there were ever a voice in full denial, that one would be it.

Of course I was going to look at the papers. Of course I wanted to hear more about the story. Of course I had nothing more pressing to do right at that moment.

And maybe, I reasoned, all that was required here was another set of eyes. Someone to see what Jordan wasn't seeing because she'd been living with the material for so long. Absent any other brilliant ideas, I wanted to see if there really could be a connection between the past and the present.

After all, one of the motives for murder? It's to keep secrets—well, *secret*. And if there was a secret hidden here, the only way it was going to be found was if I found it.

Sydney Riley, Girl Detective.

Truth be told, Jordan's documents were a mess, and I could only think she didn't have her mind—or heart—entirely on what she was doing. All the more reason for me to tidy up after her, right?

I found Callie's documents, or at least some of them, straight away: they were sitting on top of the mess, dark photocopies with halting handwriting, not at all easy to read. Or maybe that was just me; Ali and Mirela both keep saying I should be thinking about getting glasses.

The papers didn't seem to be in any particular order, and so it was that I happened upon journal pages first.

Not a day goes by that I don't miss her. Especially now. It seems—dare I say it?—cowardly, somehow, that she decided not to come the final bit of the journey with me. All along the route it was Sarah kept my spirits up. When we almost were caught right out of the gates, on the road out of Fairchild, it was Sarah held me tight, when all I wanted to do was bolt like a scared rabbit out of that shed, and that would have been the end of us. And so many other times that I finally now can write about, now I have the luxury of pen and paper and time. Too many to name. Crossing that river in the dark, and John slipping out into the current, and none of us able to reach him in time. I wept for John, and for Hattie who got caught by the trader up in Pennsylvania, but most of all, my sister, I weep for the loss of you.

Why did you do it?

Oh, God. Sarah's suicide. I hadn't stopped to think what kind of toll that would have taken on Callie. They had probably been everything to each other; Callie must have felt like it was a piece of herself, a piece of her heart, that was missing. Not unlike how her great-great-granddaughter was feeling just about now.

I read through it again: more names to mourn. The unknown John and the unknown Hattie. They'd had Callie to mourn them. That had to count for something.

The other name that caught my attention? Fairchild. Was that a city? Keeping the journal page in one hand, I used the other to thumb through the pile of notes in front of me, most of them printouts from websites, scanning them for the name, and that was where I found it. Fairchild Plantation.

Bingo. Back to the journal.

They're good to me here. It wouldn't matter if they weren't: at least they were never going to be taking a whip to me, and that's enough happiness to keep me going. Seems strange to see a whole place filled with people who look just like me. It's like the slave quarters

*from back home on Fairchild transformed themselves
into a town, but a real town, a town where no one belongs to no one else.*

*I met a fine man called Ethan a few days back,
and Maggie says he's fixing to court me. I laughed at
the idea. This baby, I said to Maggie, this baby's going
to be mulatto, ain't no decent self-respecting free man
going to want to take that on. She said, then you don't
know Ethan.*

Wait—what? I supposed I should have
seen that one coming. A mulatto child—that's
what they called someone of mixed race, back
then—could only mean one thing: Callie had
arrived in Halifax pregnant with a child whose
father was, in all probability, someone from
the white family that owned the plantation.
Fairchild Plantation.

I wondered if the pregnancy had made the
pursuers chasing the runaway slaves more ar-
dent, or less so.

Probably they didn't know. She might have
run before her pregnancy was showing. How
long did it take to travel from Virginia to Massachusetts, traveling by night, skirting popu-
lated areas? Traveling as slowly as necessary to
avoid detection, long hot days spent in hiding

places, long nights trudging through swamps and climbing hills, hearing the noises in the dark and not knowing which one might be coming for you?

Talk about taking the long way home.

Hadn't Jordan said Callie and her husband had had five children, but only the oldest one had lived? And didn't that mean that Jordan's great-great-grandfather wasn't this Ethan character at all, but a slave-owner?

Turns out nobody here can read, nor write. It's a mixed group of folk, some escaped slaves like me and Maggie, some come up from the Caribbean, some even from Africa. That's where we get our name, Africville. I told Maggie I'm going to set me up a school for these children, so they can have better lives than us. They'll be able to read books.

Ethan says, and where will we get them books? He's more concerned with building things with his hands, not interested in books. And we need him, we need them houses and more. But we need books, too. We'll figure it out. We can do anything we set our minds to. Look how fast that church went up, I said to Ethan, and praise the Lord it's true.

I told Ethan he don't have to give this baby his name, not if he don't feel it, but two things I will promise: this baby's going to be baptized in that church, and this baby's going to be free.

This baby's going to be free.

I couldn't imagine the feeling she'd had, writing those words. Thinking that thought. Even envisioning that future, knowing its shape, what it might look like. Callie had made it all the way to freedom and then some.

Wanted this to be a girl so I could name her for Sarah, keep the name alive, her living on through my blood, but baby came early and he was a boy, screaming and hollering his way into the world. Ethan couldn't love him more it were his own son instead of this light-skinned baby with the strange blue eyes. Named him Freeman. Don't care if it's not a proper name, at Fairchild we were all called whatever they took their pleasure to calling us.

Ethan don't understand that, he was born here in freedom. He's poor, but he never had no master to own him and do what he likes with him. I tried to make him understand what that means to me. Not having no master.

Our son will be the same.

Sarah came to me last night in a dream to say she's all right, she's living with Jesus now. She sang me to sleep, same as she did when we were babies together, Sarah always taking care of me, up until she couldn't take care of herself no more. I know she went into the water on purpose. She saw she got me as far up the line as she could, last leg of the journey, approaching the last stop on the railroad, and then she put it all down.

Freeman is going to know all about his aunt.

I glanced at my watch. Still some time. I thought for a moment, wondering if Jordan's laptop was password-protected. Nothing ventured, nothing gained. I opened it and a Chrome browser popped up. "Fairchild Plantation," I typed, then, after thinking about it for a moment, I added, "Virginia."

No worries there: Fairchild wasn't just a substantial plantation, I read; it was one of the first established, before Virginia even became a commonwealth. "Fairchild tells the story of the Cavendish family, eyewitnesses to eleven generations of American history. To this day, the eleventh generation continues to own, operate, and work this grand southern plantation.

Today, Fairchild is still a working plantation, a private family home, a growing business, a national historic landmark, and it provides a direct link between the past and the present."

It was still standing and, apparently, the eleventh generation had had enough of carrying on the legacy of this "grand southern plantation," because in fact it had just been sold.

By its owner.

Howard Cavendish Carter.

13

I felt a little duped.

So here we were. Jordan Bellefort was the descendant of a slave who had escaped from a plantation that just happened to be owned by Howard Carter's ancestors.

They had both traveled to a relatively obscure summer village in the off-season, far from their respective homes, at precisely the same time, and were staying at the same inn.

Unlike TV detectives, I really do believe in coincidence. For starters, we wouldn't have a word for it if such a thing didn't actually exist. Besides that—well, the world is a wild and unruly place, and randomness does occur, and does with some frequency.

But even for someone like me, there's a point at which something has been staring you in the face for long enough that you have to give in and admit it's not a coincidence at all.

I reach that point a lot later than most people. The hashtag under my name is #SoGullible. Which is why I was feeling a little duped. One or both of these people had been lying to me all along.

And damn it, I'd even *liked* both of them. In different ways, of course. But I liked them. Had they been using me? Why? How would that gain them anything? Were they working together at something they didn't want me to know about? Again, why?

And what were they both doing here?

I leaned back in the chair and shut my eyes. There was something here I wasn't getting.

My phone vibrated; a text from Mirela. *We are almost finished. I need to talk to you.*

I sighed, not wanting the distraction. I texted back. *Now?*

Little floating dots appeared on my screen, indicating Mirela was typing. Nothing happened. The little dots disappeared. She must have gotten distracted. If she needed to talk to me, she'd call.

And I had enough puzzles in front of me to keep myself occupied at least until she got back from Sandwich.

I flipped through the papers, squinted at the laptop display, felt like there was something there, some creature, some truth, lurking in the room with me, ready to reveal itself if I could just find the right key, the way in. Too many people were either in the right place at the right time—or in the wrong place at the wrong time. I didn't even know which it was.

I finally said it out loud. "Why? Why is Howard here? At the same time as Jordan?"

Behind me, the breath of air I'd thought I'd felt took shape, and Howard Carter said, "It's quite simple. Restitution."

***

I didn't turn around. "So. Howard. You aren't really planning to get married, are you?" I asked.

He sighed and shuffled in past me. He was still, I noted, using the cane. "Do you mind if I sit down?"

I make a halfhearted gesture toward one of the other chairs. He pulled it out and lowered himself, slowly and, I thought, painfully. He peered through the dark glasses at the mess on the table and nodded, as though it were confirming something for him. Possibly it was. "No, and I feel bad as heck about that, to tell you the truth. I'm not a lying man by nature, no, I am not. It just seemed the best excuse to have come here."

"There is no Lydia."

He nodded. "There is no Lydia," he agreed.

"I should've known," I said. "She never felt real. And looking back now, I didn't ask you why you'd chosen Provincetown of all places for your wedding, since you had no connection to it, and forgive me, but you aren't gay." I looked at him "You *aren't* gay, are you?" Maybe I was getting *everything* wrong here. I was starting to lose respect for my own perceptivity and insight. Or, of course, the lack thereof.

He gave a small smile. "No, ma'am, I'm not."

"So there it is. I'm completely stupid."

He started to reach across the table as though to touch me, but I jerked my arm away and he leaned back again. "It's not you, Miss— Sydney. Ma'am. I have to confess to having prevaricated, and it taxed me sorely, I can tell you. But it was I who led you astray. You had a lot on your mind, what with the murder and weddings and all. I know it couldn't last, you bein' such a smart thing and all."

I looked at him sharply. "Did you do it?"

"Do what?"

"Kill her. Kill Reggie Sanborn."

He looked startled. "Good heavens! Of course not! Sydney, I'd never hurt a fly, and that's the God's honest truth. And especially not Dr. Sanborn! She was helping me. I'd never hurt that fine lady."

"Helping you?" I frowned. "Howard. I'm lost. Start at the beginning." I hesitated. "What did you mean by restitution?"

But I thought I already knew.

He was quiet for a moment, as though marshaling his thoughts. "I was married," he said at length. "Margaret, her name was, not Lydia. Pretty as a peach. I'll never marry again, I do declare. Margaret was the love of my life, truly she was. Fractious, mind you. That woman could start an argument in an empty house! But beautiful and..." He didn't finish the sentence. There was an uncomfortable pause, and just as I was trying to figure out what to say next, he picked up one of the printouts. "I see you've been doing some reading. You've taken a look at my old home. Beautiful place, I declare it is." He looked up at me. I wished I could read his eyes behind the sunglasses. "So you can imagine what our life was like together. It was... very pleasant."

Yeah, if you can talk about a mansion in the middle of a plantation and all the money you'll ever need *pleasant*. I could stand a little of that kind of pleasant.

Howard was on his own track. "I inherited, as you probably know, a sizeable chunk of Virginia, and, fortunately, enough money to keep it maintained and us living in style. It was a good life. It was not a thoughtful life, you understand; not an examined life." He paused. "Neither of us had been raised to be particularly thoughtful."

"What *were* you raised to be?"

He smiled, a little frostily. "Wealthy, Sydney. We were raised to be wealthy."

There was a moment of silence as we both thought about that. My parents live in a Stepford-like community in New Hampshire where everyone has a landscaping company to do their lawns and caterers to do their parties and cleaners to do their chores. I think of them as wealthy. I had a feeling they weren't in the same ballpark as Howard and Margaret.

I took refuge in Julie's mantra. "So what changed?"

"Ah, yes. Now I remember that about you. Straight to the point." He sighed. "*We* changed, Sydney, ma'am. That's what changed. I'd like to say it happened all at once, out of the blue, like a revelation. But as I've gotten older—well, I'm not positive life works that way. The good Lord didn't drop a tablet our way to tell us what to do. There were a series of things that happened... first..." He stopped, apparently consulting his inner man. Or perhaps the ghost of his dead wife. Apparently he got an answer. "I will tell you what happened," he said. "I was raised by a Black woman. It still happened a great deal in the South, back when I was a boy. You northern-ers would call her a nanny, I suppose. She was everything to me."

I had the sense to stay still and say nothing.

"She had a boy of her own. Caleb, his name was. I didn't like thinking about Caleb, no, siree, I didn't. Jealous of him, you might say. I wanted to be the only apple of her eye. And then Caleb got sick, sudden-like, during the night. Her and his daddy got Caleb to the hospital, all right, but they made them wait un-til all the white people were seen to." He glanced up at me. "This was a lot of years ago, remember, ma'am. And Caleb—well, Caleb

219

died. But that wasn't the worst." Another pause, and then he said it. "The worst was when my father said, *it don't matter, they're still young, plenty more where he came from.*"

There was a moment of silence. I didn't know how to respond.

Howard drew his handkerchief across his mouth. "I will tell you the God's honest truth, I was glad when Caleb died," he said soberly. "I thought I'd have her all to myself. But when my father said that—I don't know, Miss—Sydney. Like something inside me woke up." He wasn't looking at me. "And then I married my Margaret. And she did like her clothes—whoo-whee, that woman could shop for clothes! Sooner or later, though, she'd get tired of 'em. Next season sort of thing. Had to make room in her closets for more. She sometimes gave her cast-offs to the help." He glanced up as though challenging me to question his word choice. "And there was one dress, oh, Margaret thought mighty highly of that dress, she did. It was a beautiful evening gown, pearls all over it, because back then we still did go to parties where you had to dress up."

Howard cleared his throat. "Anyway, the long and short of it is, Margaret gave that dress to her maid to wear for her wedding."

220

Another pause. Another silence.

"Well, the long and short of that was that someone accused that poor girl of stealing that dress, and they accused her husband—husband of only a few hours, mind you—of havin' been in Margaret's rooms to get that dress. Didn't even bother to ask us. Margaret didn't even know. But they strung him up anyway."

His expression was bleak. "All over a dress. Just a dress. And that woke me up, Sydney, ma'am. The truth of the matter is, I was just as entitled, just as downright mean, as any of my forebears. I came to that realization slowly, as did my wife. We talked about it, for months we talked about it. We talked about Caleb. We talked about that young man married Margaret's maid. And finally we found some of what you might call moral clarity. It didn't come easy, and it didn't come early, but it came all the same."

Another pause. I didn't know if it was the lighting or if he really did look pale.

"Having moral clarity is not enough," Howard said. "Margaret kept saying it: we had to act."

Somehow I couldn't see Howard protesting in the streets. He was more of a behind-the-scenes kind of guy. "How?"

"I'll tell you something I have come to believe, Sydney, ma'am. I believe people of color—and I will tell you something else, I used to call them colored people, and not think anything of it—I now believe people of color in this country are owed. Literally owed." He sighed. "I don't have to take you to school. People like me, we're responsible for makin' sure Black people stayed in their place. The place *we* put them in. Not enough of anything—food, shelter, education, opportunity. Margaret kept saying they didn't have hall passes to the American Way of Life." He smiled at the memory. "She had a way with words, Margaret did. She believed—we believed—that something should be done about it."

He was wheezing a little. I wished there were a window I could open for him. "Sorry for the soapbox, Sydney, ma'am, but it has to be said. Has to be said out loud. no matter who it inconveniences. Everything they have, my people stole. From at least six or seven generations of people who just happen to look different from us. How can anyone live with that?"

"I've heard debates about reparations," I said, a little uncertainly. "I can't remember everything I heard. I don't know how it would work."

I wasn't sure he'd heard me; he was pursuing his own journey through the past. "It should be done on a national level, of course," he said thoughtfully. "Perhaps one day it will. I have to say, I'm an optimist. I have high hopes for this country, ma'am. But it's just not happening fast enough for me."

I was still stuck on the logistics of a national level of compensation. "But reparations—isn't that hard to do? To figure out?"

"Do you think so?" He removed his sunglasses and put them on the table; his eyes were watery. "Well, now. We've offered reparations to Native Americans, to Japanese-Americans, even helped rebuild Europe as part of the Marshall Plan. It can be done, when we decide to do it. When they decide to do anything, Americans are unstoppable."

"So you think the government should be compensating people," I said. This was devolving quickly into a history lesson, and I had a creeping feeling—call it a premonition—that we were getting short on time.

"Yes," said Howard simply. "Anyone can trace their heritage to people who were enslaved? They should get money. Financial compensation. It's that simple."

I had a feeling it wasn't. "Okay. But—forgive me, Howard—you're not in Washington advocating for reparations. This is about something different. This is personal. Why don't you just tell me?"

He reached into a pocket and pulled out his wallet, spent a moment sorting through what was in there, then removed a photograph and slid it across the table to me. Of course Howard wouldn't keep his photographs on his mobile phone. "My Margaret," he said.

A middle-aged, pleasant-looking white woman sitting at an outdoor table, umbrella overhead, vast green lawn stretching out all around her. Flowered dress, floppy hat. Iced tea on the table. An aging Southern belle. "She's lovely," I said, handing the photograph back. I wasn't sure what I was supposed to be understanding here..

Howard took the photo and, to my surprise, gently kissed it before replacing it in his wallet. "She was," he said sadly, "a lady."

I let that sit for a moment, then asked, "When did you lose her, Howard?" Might as well do the hard part; he was the one who'd opened the door. Spread it wide, even.

He put the wallet away. "A year ago, in July," he said. "Hottest day of the year, it was. I remember the heat."

As far as I was concerned, Virginia itself was the hottest day of the year, any year. So that July had to have been memorable. "I'm sorry for your loss," I said.

He nodded. "I've been rambling, Sydney, ma'am, and I'm sorry for that. But I just wanted to give you a glimpse of—of the background to what I'm going to tell you."

"Context," I agreed, nodding.

"Context," he said, as though trying out the word. He pursed his lips around it. "Context. Yes. Well. As I said, it was not a moment of clarity that came to us, just a lot of late-night talks, reading, listening to other people. Fairchild might not have been run on the backs of slaves anymore, but nearly everyone who worked there was Black. I had to look at that. I had to listen to them." He sighed. "Margaret was becoming impatient. She knew, long before I did, that she was—ill. She did not speak of it until it was impossible not to. And she said we couldn't wait. That's what Margaret said. So we decided, if they aren't going to do it in time, then we will."

"Your own reparations," I said. "Personal ones." I was following along now, the path stretching out ahead of us, bright and sparkling with certainty and something else I couldn't quite define.

He nodded. "Hired an investigative firm," he said. "Good fellows, they were, every one of them. Worked faster than a knife through butter, I'll say that for them."

"What were they looking for, Howard? Exactly?"

He looked surprised that I wasn't understanding. "For whoever should be the ones to own Fairchild," he said. "What else? We didn't deserve it, Margaret and me. But we knew someone out there must. Maybe one person, maybe a lot of people. There was enough to go around." He thought for a moment. "Now, we're goin' back a ways," he said. "My great-great-great grandfather. Josiah Carter. Turning out cotton like there was no tomorrow. Got rich as all-get-out. Had children, and sickly things they were. Lost a lot of them. Heartache to him, must have been. Only one son survived."

I shivered; I couldn't help it. An odd parallel with Callie's life: one son, many deaths.

"That son, Howard by name—we're traditionalists in my family, you see, Sydney—inherited the plantation, passed it on to my grandfather, so on. Strange family, the Carters. Not much good in the procreation department. Margaret and me, we couldn't have children, not a-tall."

"I'm sorry," I said automatically.

Howard shook his head. "Don't really matter now, do it?" he said softly. "I reckon it's all for the best. But back to old Josiah, now. Bit of a pickle, he was in, on account of going blind at a young age. His mother had inherited the plantation—that's when the name changed, Cavendish to Carter—and there'd been some sort of accident with her when he was young. We never got the whole story of what happened, no, ma'am, but while she was still alive she babied him, him being disabled, as we'd say now, and all." He paused to breathe for a moment. "Like I said, all well and good when his parents were there, but he had to learn to run the plantation on his own. So while he was doing that, he didn't learn that system they had, teaching blind people to read. Braille. And Josiah? He was a man of great intellectual curiosity. He reached out to the world. He had a library full of books—no offense to you, Sydney, ma'am, but at least five times the size of this one—and he wanted to read them all. Lookin' for learning, he was. Books unlocked the world."

"Which he couldn't do," I said.

He nodded. "I see you know where my story is heading," he said. "My agency, they tracked it all down. The girl that was there every day, reading to him, the classics, Adam Smith, *Walden, Moby-Dick,* what have you. More'n I've ever read, to tell you the honest truth. I haven't been the reader I might have been. Too late now. There wasn't anything he didn't want her to read to him, and that went on for years, from when she was no mor'n a little girl. And two things happened. One, this girl—her name was Callie, by the way, though I reckon you already know that—this girl Callie, she got herself an education, reading these books aloud, day after day."

I was seeing Callie in a new light. No wonder she'd become such a guiding energy in Africville. It wasn't that she could simply read and write. She had an array of knowledge that offered her the opportunity to make sense of the world. Contextually. Intellectually.

"And the other thing is, spending time together like that, they became close. Not like equals-close, that wouldn't have happened, but close."

"Close enough for her to become pregnant," I said. Even to my own ears, my voice sounded bitter.

"Yes," said Howard. "That close."

We sat with it for a moment.

"What happened to Sarah?" I sked.

"The sister? Yes. Well." He paused. "I'm not one to reckon I can get into another person's mind, no, ma'am, but as my agents tell me, she did work in the house with her sister, and she did become with child around the same time. I imagine the household was close. I imagine—"

"No," I interrupted. "Stop right there. You're not going to say that it could have been consensual."

He shook his head. "Probably not," he conceded. "And it's true that the ladies—felt they had to leave."

"Had to escape, you mean?"

He sighed. He was getting tired. "The point is, they found out about Callie. The agency I hired. And about her son, Freedom. And about his daughter, Amelie. And about her daughter, Bella. And about her daughter, Jordan."

I narrowed my eyes. "That's all? Just that one straight line? No errant cousins? No other branches of the family tree? No black sheep?"

He looked at me gravely. "There have been," he said. "No one who's survived."

"So you got in touch with Jordan."

"I did. I fear she had some—misapprehensions about my intentions. We worked that out, though, yes, ma'am. Margaret was still alive then. Her regret was she'd never meet Miss Bellefort. Nor, indeed, Dr. Sanborn." He relaxed a little, smiled. "They had only been married a short while before we began our correspondence," he said. "That was—a challenge for Margaret and me, it has to be said. A married couple that was—women. Never even thought about that sort of thing before, truth be told. It wasn't something we'd encountered before."

"You seem to have come to terms with it."

"So we did. So we did. It's been a revealing time for us, I don't mind telling you. And we spoke to our lawyers, who were all for making it all more difficult than it had to be. But that's what they're like, isn't it? Complicatin' things all the time."

"What, exactly, is it you were asking for? What were they complicating?" I was feeling slightly adrift.

He looked startled. "Well, Sydney. I thought that was clear. We wanted to give Miss Bellefort and Dr. Sanborn our money, of course!"

I hadn't exactly *not* expected it, but it was still like a punch. The sale of the plantation. Restitution for something long gone badly wrong. Reparations for generations of abuse. "The government wasn't doing it..." I said slowly.

He nodded. "We couldn't help everybody," he explained. "And we weren't in a position to influence politicians—I've made it a practice to stay as far away from that bunch of jackasses as I can. So there were a lot of ways we couldn't help, and a lot of people we couldn't help. But we *could* do something about our own family, leastways, that's how we saw it. And our family was Miss Bellefort and Dr. Sanborn." He paused and, for the first time, said, "Jordan and Regina."

"But Reggie wasn't technically your family," I said.

He looked shocked. "You surprise me," he said. "Of course she was. She was the one, more than anyone, who showed me that the past—it doesn't have to be an indicator of the future." He paused, working it out. "What Regina did with her life, that showed me how a single person can do good. Her life—she was everything I wasn't. Everything I hadn't been. I was maybe makin' up for that, for who I'd been, giving in the envelope at church every Sunday and leavin' it at that. The point of giving something away isn't so you can say how it will be used. No, siree. The point is to let the recipient do what they want with it. But I have to confess—I *liked* knowing that the money would come full circle. I liked that a lot. Margaret did, too. Kept saying Regina was living our best lives for us." He stopped, the handkerchief at his mouth again. "Not a day goes by I don't miss that woman. Not a day. So that's when I decided to do it in person. We wrote—well, my attorneys wrote—to Jordan. I didn't want to go to Canada." He touched the handkerchief to his lips again. "To tell you the truth, I couldn't have gone to Canada. Too much stress. New England seems foreign enough to me! Margaret and me, we were homebodies. Never even got ourselves passports. Didn't like to leave the house." *If a hundred-thousand-acre plantation can be described as the house.* "Margaret said it would be good to travel, for us to do it somewhere else. The handing-over, you see. That wasn't going to be exactly popular in our neck of the woods."

Wait. That brought out a whole new area of inquiry. Had someone found out about the sale, and Howard's intentions? Had someone felt they deserved it more than Jordan and Reggie?

Oblivious to my thoughts, Howard was still talking. "And Provincetown has always been of particular interest." He caught my look. "Amateur historian, I've become, yes, ma'am, since this all started. Once we knew where Miss Callie had gone on her way to Canada, well, I looked into it. Your history, I mean." I must have looked startled, because he chuckled. "Not yours, though I'm sure it's fascinating. No, I'm talking about Provincetown. About the town's history. About the Pilgrims, and the Mayflower. And about that poor lady, Mrs. Bradford."

I stared at him. "Dorothy Bradford?" How did *she* come into all this?

"Such a sad thing. Disappearing like that off the ship. A lot like poor Callie's sister Sarah, disappearing off that fishing boat. Strange parallel there, I thought, and Margaret agreed.

233

We thought we'd make a trip of it. Pay our respects, we reckoned, to both of them. Thought as long as we were going to meet the ladies, might as well do it here. I'm attracted to women with sad histories, it would seem." He paused. "And then Jordan said she could get a job here, just like that, singing at your women's festival. To be perfectly honest, Sydney, it felt as though it was *meant*, us all bring here Ordained, somehow. Margaret was going to try and make the journey, too. They were all excited. But, really, it was Regina's reaction that tickled me pink, because of her involvement in that heritage site up there, a place for people to learn something. Changing the world, yes, ma'am. And there was a neighborhood clinic… Margaret and me, we couldn't have been happier. It just seemed appropriate, we reckoned. Money from slavery going to teach people about slavery. Keep that place Africville going for another hundred years. Seems like a fitting legacy, now that both Regina and Margaret have passed."

No legacy, I thought, excused a murder.

I looked at Howard. He'd come alive, talking about his Margaret. And the reparations. "So," I said softly, "who killed Reggie?"

He looked at me blankly. "I have no idea," he said. "I thought *you* knew."

14

S ome things were making sense. Others seemed to be slipping completely out of my grasp, sliding like water through my clutching fingers.

Why hadn't Jordan told me the real reason she was in Provincetown? I had no doubt she'd told a partial truth, that she was here to research Callie and Sarah and the Underground Railroad, and that Billy had arranged for her to sing to make the trip worthwhile... but talk about worthwhile. I'll be honest, if someone had just gifted me a big chunk of the Commonwealth of Virginia and had come to do the paperwork with me, that's something that wouldn't have slipped my mind to mention. Might even have talked about it. Might even be an occasion for celebration; but that's just me. Others' mileage might vary.

What I knew was that, medical examiner or no medical examiner, Jordan needed to have some conversations when she got back. With me. With Julie. With Howard.

Howard. "Wait," I said. "Have you even *spoken* to Jordan since you got here?" I'd only ever seen either of them alone.

He shook his head. "We were in touch, before, of course," he said. "But when I arrived... well, we'd arranged to meet at the Race Point Inn after Women's Week was over. I didn't want to get in the way. We were going to meet up on Sunday, only I was—well, I'll admit, I was impatient. And anxious. Wanting to get the lay of the land. Still didn't want to interrupt her—and then of course later learned what had happened to Regina." He touched the handkerchief to his lips. "She knew I'd be coming here," he said again. "We selected your—establishment—on purpose. It represented the confluence of our lives, yes, ma'am, Miss Callie being sheltered here before going on for the remainder of her journey. It seemed apt." A long pause. "I thought discretion would be the best approach. I thought I'd wait until she contacted me, that she'd be in touch once she was ready. After all, I have all the time in the world."

He didn't look like he had all the time in the world. He looked like he didn't have five minutes to spare; his skin was gray, taut, his eyes exhausted.

I didn't want to rock his boat, which seemed rocky enough. "But, Howard, it just seems odd to me that you both have come from so far to see each other, and you're both in the same building, and you haven't even bumped into each other." I was sure he was still hiding something from me. He seemed to be having troubles meeting my eyes, which could mean a lot of things, but it felt evasive. I was starting to pay attention to what my body was telling me, and the coldness in my stomach that had started when I found Howard's name among Jordan's papers hadn't abated. There was something here I wasn't getting.

Not yet.

My phone kept buzzing, and I kept silencing it. The display wasn't a number I recognized, which could mean anything—someone new trying to arrange a wedding, someone confirming or canceling an appointment, or even (now that I knew the full extent of her deviousness) my mother borrowing someone else's phone to trick me into answering. I wasn't taking chances on the latter, and I didn't have time for the former. It's why God created voicemail.

I closed out of Jordan's browser and shut the laptop cover. "Howard," I said, "Somehow your little reunion with Jordan has had unanticipated consequences. You need to speak to the police. You need to tell them all this—about planning to meet them here, about selling your estate, everything. I don't know how, but Reggie got killed because she came here, and she came here because she was meeting you."

"I wasn't at the dinner—"

"And I'm not saying you were, and I'm not saying you killed her," I said, quickly. "But all of this is part of it, somehow, don't you see that? Julie Agassi—she's a police detective here in town—she has to know. The state police will have to know." But even as I said it, I realized how little there was to understand here. There was a correlation I just wasn't seeing. How in the world were these old secrets and a new murder connected?

My telephone rang again.

Howard sighed, and I felt the heaviness, the tiredness emanating from him. "Yes, of course I will," he said. His eyes met mine. "I was trying to do something good," he said, a quaver behind the words. Howard had come a long way—literally and metaphorically—to have his good deed blow up in his face.

In Reggie's face.

"And you need to go ahead and meet with Jordan," I said. "She needs something positive and beautiful in her life right now. She's on her way back from the medical examiner's office. She needs something to look forward to. You can't wait for her to come to you."

He nodded. "I think we've come to the point where we need each other, yes, indeed, I do," he said.

***

I finished tidying up—it was, after all, my excuse for going into the library in the first place—and left Jordan's research work in neat piles on top of and around her computer. Howard decided to go and lie down until Jordan got back from Sandwich, and made me promise no fewer than three times that I would call him as soon as she arrived.

I locked the library door. We're not big on locking things here in P'town—if there's a key to my apartment I haven't a clue where it is—

but this was private material, not for other guests to peruse.

Not that I'd had a right to peruse it, either, as I had a feeling everyone I knew was going to tell me. What's that phrase about it being easier to ask for forgiveness than permission?

I was downstairs and heading to Mike's office when the phone rang yet again, and I lost all patience. If this was my mother… "What?" I snapped. I don't think I'd ever answered a telephone that way before.

"Sydney! Thank God you have answered."

It was Mirela, and there was disaster in her voice.

15

There was a click, and another voice came on. "Sydney. You're a hard person to get hold of. You've kept us waiting."

"Who is this?" I asked. The question was automatic; I was pretty sure I already knew.

"I think you already know," confirmed Billy Thompson. "And you need to listen closely, because your friend from—" He broke off for a moment, and I could hear his voice, muffled: "Where're you from, anyway?"

Mirela's voice, close by. "Bulgaria," she said.

"That's the one," said Billy, and brought his voice closer to the phone again. "You heard her. Your friend from Bulgaria is here with me, and you wouldn't want anything bad to happen to her."

I opened Mike's office door; no time for niceties like knocking. He wasn't there, but I slipped in anyway and closed the door behind me. I had a feeling I was going to need some privacy for this call. "Where are you?" I asked. "What do you want?" I could feel my pulse accelerate and my breath go ragged, and I wondered for a moment if I was going to have one of Howard's panic attacks. *Not helpful, Riley. Breathe. Just breathe.*

Billy laughed. It was an unpleasant sound. "See, that's what I like," he said. "We're interested in the same subjects. I was about to tell you where we are. What I want? That will have to wait a little, eh?" First time he'd sounded really Canadian to me. Maybe he was under stress.

Maybe he was perfectly in his element.

"So tell me where you are, then," I said. "I'll come."

He sighed. "See, it's not that easy, Sydney. I wish it were. It's not that I don't trust you, but I don't trust you. I know you're pals with a cop in town. And I wouldn't want her crashing the party."

Breathing was really getting more difficult. "I won't bring Julie," I said. "I don't want you to hurt Mirela." Thoughts flashing like lights through my head. Mirela had been with Jordan in Sandwich. She said she wanted to talk to me. Now she was with Billy. What had he done to Jordan? Had he meant to kill both her and Reggie all along? "Just tell me," I said.

"You have to do a couple of things for me first," said Billy. "And I think it would be better for Mirela, really I do, if you could do them quickly."

"I will," I said. "Just don't hurt her. Please don't. I'll do whatever you want."

"Yes," said Billy. "I know you will." He let me sit with that for a moment, then said, "Mr. Howard Carter is staying at your inn. He has some paperwork he brought to Provincetown with him. Some very special paperwork. I think by now you probably know what it's about."

"Yes," I said. He had to be holding Jordan as well as Mirela. If she were still alive.

"Good. Glad you didn't argue. Glad you didn't pretend you don't know what I'm talking about. He must have gotten you up to speed on the whole thing."

"Transferring a fortune," I said.

"That's the one," he agreed.

"What about it?"

"Well, now, I'd like to see Mr. Howard Carter and his paperwork. And I'd like you to bring him here."

Breathe, Riley. "Howard is not in good shape," I began. "He had a panic—"

"—attack this morning. Yeah, I know. Your point?"

Was it only this morning? "I don't think he can go anywhere," I said.

"Now, see, that's not good. I thought you wanted to help your friend Mirela. You're not sounding very helpful to me." He paused. "Did I mention her little girl? No? Her little girl's here with us, too." His voice got muffled again. "What's her name?"

Mirela said, "Lily."

"Lily. That's right. Cute baby. Thanks, hon." I could just imagine the expression on Mirela's face; no one calls her hon. On the other hand, she had more to deal with than worrying about names.

My mind was wandering; I needed to focus. "I'm not trying to be difficult," I said. "I'll come, of course I'll come. I can get the paperwork from Howard. He can sign it and I'll bring it to you." And then what? Was he going to force Jordan to sign it over to him? None of this would hold in court; didn't you need a lawyer or a notary or someone to make signatures valid?

Wandering again.

"Nice try, Sydney. Sorry, but no go. I need you and Howard to come together. No one else. You call the police, the little girl dies. You bring anyone else with you, the little girl dies. You tell anyone where you're going, the little girl dies. Got that?"

I swallowed. "Yes."

"Okay. Drive to the Snail Road entrance to the Seashore."

"Wait," I said, incredulous. "You're in the *dunes*?"

Coastal dunes make up roughly one-third of the Cape Cod National Seashore, They're a major factor of life in Provincetown: anyone who has a dog knows them well, and in-season Art's Dune Tours takes people out to see them and gawk at the dune shacks, tiny weathered gray cottages that are remnants of the past, of poets and artists who sought the stark inspiration offered by isolated, windswept dunes on the back beach.

This side of the Seashore doesn't have bike trails or greasy fried seafood stands, no easily accessible beaches and a hefty climb to get anywhere—even a healthy person's calves ache after tramping up and down sand. They are undeniably beautiful—windswept, sunlit shadowy dunes with patches of evergreens and grasses rolling off toward the blue sea—but they were no place for Howard.

On the other hand, I could totally understand Billy's choice. If you're on top of a high dune, you can see for miles around, certainly whether or not anyone uninvited is on their way. And even if someone were to flounder into view, there would be plenty of time to deal with them.

Billy said, "Got it in one. I want you to park at Snail Road and come in that way. We're about half a mile in."

"No," I said. "He can't. Seriously. Listen to me, I'm not being difficult on purpose, this is physics." *Physics, Riley?* "He can't handle stairs, how do you think he's getting into the dunes?" Coming at them from the Snail Road entrance off Route Six was especially challenging: the first thing you come upon is a sand hill that looks a little like the sheer edge of a building. It is long, and it is steep, and on a good day I can barely make it up. Howard wouldn't last ten seconds. "He just can't," I said to Billy, a little despairingly. "Listen, I'll do anything. I'll bring the papers. I'll swear him to silence.

Or he can come in the car and wait for me. Whatever. But he seriously can't do the dunes." He didn't say anything, and I plunged on. "Think about it! You just climbed in yourself," I said. "You're young and strong and it still had to have been an effort. He's an old man and he's unwell. Don't ask for something you *know* can't happen."

Silence. I strained, listening hard in case I could hear Mirela, or even Lily. Nothing. *Breathe...*

"All right," said Billy at last. "He comes with you. He sits in the car. No phones. No computers. You bring anything and your friend and her little girl both die."

"Okay," I said quickly, before he could change his mind. "It will take a few minutes. I have to go up to the Monument to fetch my car. Howard has to get ready."

"You have half an hour. Bring the papers with you." He clicked off.

Holy Mary, I thought in despair. How could I get all that done in half an hour? On impulse, I hit Ali's icon on my phone. Maybe, just maybe he was in a place he could answer... No. Voicemail. There were other people I could call. Karen, Ali's sister, who was the Boston police commissioner. Julie Agassi.

Glenn or Mike, who were both sensible and also loved Mirela. I even had an absurd impulse to call my mother.

Half an hour.

Holy holy holy, just the one word, begging for help from a God I'd certainly been neglecting of late. I tore up to the Harry Kemp Suite, pounding on the door. "Howard! Howard!"

It seemed to take forever for him to open the door, though it probably was less than a minute. A minute I didn't have to spare. "Miss Sydney, ma'am?" The voice was querulous, an old man's voice: Howard had aged in a matter of an hour. "Is that you?"

"Howard, open the door!" He unlocked it and I practically fell into the room. "I don't have time to explain. Do you have the documents—the paperwork—whatever it's called, for this transfer of your money to Jordan and Reggie?" I didn't want to even consider what had happened to Jordan.

He gestured toward the suite's desk; thank God it was all in neat folders, unlike the wild disarray in the library. He wasn't wearing his dark glasses, and was blinking like I'd woken him up. Maybe I had. "Good. Get a coat, please, and come with me. We have to take the documents with us."

"I don't understand—"

I was halfway to the desk to grab the folders myself. I whirled to face him. "Howard, listen to me," I said, and even to my ear there was an edge of something—hysteria, perhaps—in my voice. "Billy Thompson, that's Jordan's manager? He is threatening to—listen, he wants all this. Maybe he'll make her sign it over to him, I don't know. I don't know enough. But he has my friend, my best friend in the world, and her little girl, he's—he's got them." I lost it for a second, a ragged sob. "Kidnapped, or something. We have half an hour to get the papers to him, Howard, he said you have to come, too, so please *please* just get your coat and come with me!"

He was moving slowly, far too slowly. This was a man, I recalled, who'd been born into wealth. He was accustomed to having people do things for him. What he wasn't accustomed to was an urgent need for speed in a case where there wasn't someone to do his bidding. "Listen. I'm going to go get my car. Please meet me in front of the inn as quickly as you can. Howard, please!"

I grabbed the folders, willy-nilly, and ran. At least the rain had stopped; the sky was grey and washed-out, but I could see where I was going.

I'd told Howard to get a coat; I hadn't bothered with one myself. It didn't matter. The only thing that mattered was saving Mirela.

And Lily, I reminded myself; and Lily.

I was short of breath before I even hit High Pole Hill, racing down Commercial Street, dodging the few pedestrians around as I ran. No time for more self-deprecating thoughts about joining a gym: no time for much thought at all. I turned at Standish Street and ran past the Governor Bradford and Mooncusser Tattoo and flung myself at the hill. Fortunately it was off-season, which meant I'd have left the keys in the car.

By the time I got to the top I was heaving, gulping great mouthfuls of air, and my hands were trembling when I fitted the key into the ignition. The Little Green Car roared to life; *let up on the accelerator, Riley.*

I figured my time was a little more than halfway up.

I turned left onto Bradford Street and immediately got behind someone with Connecticut plates, and for the first time ever in my life as a driver, I hit the horn as the tourist crawled along. The horn, predictably, did nothing: so I did something else I never do and flew past him going up a low-visibility hill. He beeped back at me. *Good: call the cops. Please call the cops. Julie will recognize my car, and no matter how much she teases me about dead bodies, she does respect my driving; she'll know something's wrong.*

I was kidding myself. Julie wasn't coming. No one was coming. I was the cavalry.

Howard was standing in front of the inn. He'd pulled himself together and looked a great deal less lost than he had when I'd left him. He piled into the front seat and pulled the door closed fast. "Now, Sydney," he said. "Tell me what has happened here."

I was working out the fastest route in my head. Up Center Street, I decided, across Bradford to Conwell, right on Route Six to the Snail Road intersection. "It's Billy," I said. "Somehow he knows what you're all here for. He has Mirela and the baby up in the dunes. I don't know what he's done with Jordan."

"He is the individual who killed Regina?"

I nodded. "I think so. I mean, this kind of gives it away, doesn't it? Maybe he did it together with the bartender, I don't know. It has to be him." But what was his game plan? Get the paperwork signed over to him—if he was smart, he was holding Jordan somewhere else—and then… what? Send it all out to an offshore account? "How does it work?" I asked Howard. "Legally, I mean. Do you have electronic access?"

He said, blankly, "I don't know what that means. Is that the same as online banking?"

"Kind of. Same sort of thing. Once the papers are signed, can you transfer all the money at once?"

"I don't know." He shook his head. "I never asked. But it wasn't all going directly to them."

"What do you mean?" And when had Conwell Street gotten this *long*? We'd been on it forever.

"Well, the tax burden would be significant," he said. "Even though affordable, of course, for me and Margaret. We could have helped them with that. Still, I never saw sense in giving away more than you have to, aren't I right? So the initial payment was going directly."

"Directly—where?"

"Three places." He counted them on his fingers. "The Africville Historic Site. The Caspar Square neighborhood health clinic. The

Ebenezer Baptist Church. All of them, of course, in Halifax."

I pulled onto Route Six and pushed the accelerator down; the Little Green Car hesitated as though surprised and then gave me the power. "Because it could be a donation rather than an inheritance?"

He nodded. "Something like that. But the rest of it is all there, too. I think the girls were still deciding how to work it out. We were going to discuss all that here." He hadn't really cared, I diagnosed: he had made his restitution, had said his mea culpas, had provided reparations. I imagined him returning to Virginia, a lonely Christmas in some small cottage he'd allotted himself when he left Fairchild, toasting a photograph of Margaret and assuring her he'd finished everything, waiting for time to pass so he could die and join the love of his life.

Snail Road. I braked, turned left across the divided highway—no oncoming traffic—and pulled up on the side of Route Six, facing the direction in which I'd come. Ahead of me, sitting alone, was Mirela's GTE. "Sign whatever you need to sign," I said, dumping the folder on his lap. Why hadn't I checked the time? "Damn. Do you have a phone?"

"Yes, right here." He vaguely patted pockets and pulled it out. I opened my door and flung the phone as far as I could toward Mirela's car.

Howard was scratching away. "I don't think this is going to be legal—"

"I don't care," I said. I was already out of the Little Green Car and leaning in for the papers. "The key's in the ignition; turn it on if you get cold and need the heater." I grabbed the folders from him.

"Sydney—wait—"

There was no time. No time, no time, no time. Hugging the folders to my chest, I started scrambling up the dune, my blood beating loudly in my ears. Down on one knee, slipping in the sand, back up again, it had surely been half an hour by now.

Something else, too; unbidden, Jordan's voice that first night coming back to me, haunting, exquisite, flowing as if on air.

Come take my hand, for hope
is an unturned page in a book
That we're all still writing…

Jordan might be dead. Mirela and Lily were in danger. And if I didn't get this stuff to Billy… *Breathe*, I told myself, but there wasn't much breath in me to spare.

And then I was scrambling over the top of the dune and could see people out in front of me, two smaller dunes away. I waved, wildly, and shouted. "I'm here! I have it!" The wind was fierce up here, and it carried my words away, off behind me, toward Route Six and Provincetown and safety. Still, he had to see me, to know I was getting there. I plunged down the side of my dune and kept putting one foot in front of the other, running in slow motion through sand that kept shifting under my feet. I didn't dare look up. *I can do this. I can do this.*

Up another dune. The wind was intense, whipping off the ocean and across the sands, and I hadn't stopped for a coat. Halfway up the second dune I realized my teeth were chattering. It didn't matter. Mirela and Lily were all that mattered.

And then I was at the last one, my feet coming out from under me and sliding down on my bottom, sand everywhere, in my nose and mouth and eyes and hair, and still it didn't matter, it couldn't matter. There was only one thing I had to do. I had to save my friends.

Nothing else mattered.

I gasped as I hit the bottom. Somehow I'd managed to keep the folders tight against my chest, even when I was using one arm to flail and try to keep my balance. That alone was a miracle. I was close to having the air knocked out of me, and I struggled to my knees, taking in the sharp cold air in deep gasps.

My left arm, the one I'd broken, was really hurting. *Ignore it.*

Someone was talking to me, but I couldn't make it out. "Wait," I gasped. "I—need—to—breathe. Just—let—me—breathe…"

When I finally focused, Billy was standing in front of me. He looked tough and dangerous, his hair slicked back from the rain, black leather jacket and leather pants. Perfect outfit for a villain, I thought irrelevantly. Not that that was a prerequisite for anything: if he was going to shoot me, it didn't really matter how he looked when he did it.

That "shoot" was an option was clear. I could tell that from the gun in his hand.

"Sydney." I could finally hear his voice. He was standing in front of me, waving the gun in my face. Miss Manners would definitely have something to say about that. "Do you hear me?"

I nodded and gulped more air. "I—hear—you."

"Good." He didn't look like he was much happier than I was to be there. "Where's Howard Carter?"

Sitting—in my car," I said. "You told me—to bring him. I brought him." Another gulp of air. I didn't even try to stand up. Breathing was enough for now.

I finally got myself enough under control that I could look around for Mirela. She was standing a couple of yards away, hugging herself slightly, her purple suede jacket bright against the dull browns and yellows of the dunes. "Are you—are you all right?" It took me two tries to get the sentence out.

"Never mind about her," said Billy. Mirela moved her head slightly to the side and I saw past her.

Jordan Bellefort. Holding Lily. I looked at her for a moment, then said, stupidly, "But you're dead."

She might not have been dead, but someone else was: there was a youngish man lying by her feet on the sand, and I thought I vaguely recognized Jed the sometime-bartender. Maybe. He was the only person in the charmed circle I could think of who would have been invited to this little party.

Jordan was holding Lily in the classic burp-the-baby position against her left shoulder. "I don't know why you'd think that," she said. The wind caught the words and she moved a few paces closer to us. "Not when there's so much to do here, eh?"

Mirela said, "You should explain to Sydney."

"Why? Because I owe her for all her kindness to me during my time of grief?" But she was smiling. "For what it's worth, Sydney, yes, you have been very kind. I appreciate it."

Mirela said to me, loudly, "Could you hear that? This wind is very strong."

I didn't know exactly what she wanted, but I played along. "What did you say?" I yelled at Jordan.

Lily began to cry, and I felt rather than saw Mirela's body go rigid. Jordan attempted the jiggle-the-baby move with no noticeable effect. She came a few steps closer; I couldn't imagine having a child wailing in your ear was a good way to hold a conversation out in the dunes. Or anywhere, for that matter.

Not to mention being a less-than-calming influence.

Billy said, "Let's get this over with."

"We can wait a minute," Jordan said. "Sydney needs to catch her breath."

"Why did you do it?" I asked her.

She smiled; I could swear she smiled. "I've been surprised you haven't worked it out. It's simple, really," she said. "Reggie was going to give away all my money."

She was right: it was breathtakingly simple. "You didn't want it to go to Africville," I said. *Motives for murder: greed, power, lust, love. Check: greed.*

"Of course I didn't want it to go to Africville," she snapped. "I was the one owed the money. My family. My people." Reggie, I thought, had probably argued those words described the heritage foundation, and the clinic, and the church. *My family. My people.*

I heard Howard's voice in my head. "Money from slavery going to teach people." He'd been "tickled pink," he said.

Jordan hadn't been tickled any kind of color. Jordan wasn't interested in Reggie's pet projects. Jordan was interested in Jordan.

Billy was ready to move on. "Come on," he said to me, gesturing helpfully with his gun in case I didn't know what he wanted me to do. "Stand up."

The sand was moving under me every time I shifted my weight ever so slightly, and I was still clutching the paperwork against my right side. My left arm certainly wasn't going to support me trying to stand up, no matter how many physical therapy exercises I did. "I honestly don't think I can," I said.

Jordan moved closer, and as she did, she slowly pulled something out from under Lily's coat. A pistol. "Just a reminder," she said to Mirela.

Mirela didn't say a word. Didn't cry out. Just stood there.

Lily, on the other hand, had a lot to say. Lily was in fact starting to move into operatic-range crying. It was making Jordan uncomfortable. I couldn't imagine what it was doing to Mirela, but she wasn't giving anything away.

"Give me the papers," said Billy.

"Actually, don't," said Jordan. There was a pause. "I think this is as far as I want you to come, Billy." Her gun was moving away from the baby and in Billy's direction.

"What? Jordan, wait, I got you the deal—"

I glanced at Mirela, quickly, but couldn't read her.

I had to do something. This wasn't going to end well for any of us if I didn't. But sitting in a pile of sand doesn't really give you a lot of options for intervention. "Okay," I yelled. "Get your damned papers!"

I flung them as far up as my one arm could manage. I needn't have worried about Billy catching them: the wind grabbed them in a graceful rapid swirl and flung them all around us on the sand; within seconds, some were rapidly making their way toward Route Six. Billy cursed and jumped for them, and Jordan brought her pistol the rest of the way away from Lily and shot him.

The sound was still echoing around the dunes when there was another shot and Jordan was moving, falling, and I finally understood what was going on and scrambled in time to grab Lily as she fell in the deep, soft, forgiving sand.

Mirela was standing very still with a very small pistol in her hand, still pointing where Jordan had been standing, her face still not betraying anything.

"Damn," I said. "Am I the only one here without one of those?"

16

I was still trying to explain to Ali why our goddaughter was staying with me.

"Julie says of course Mirela will be cleared, it was self-defense, but until then, the child protective people don't want a kid in her care. And of course she doesn't have any official adoption papers or anything…"

"I can't believe you're living with a six-month-old," he said. "I would pay good money to be able to watch this."

I wasn't sure I really believed it, either. The police had arrived when—it seemed—the sound of the gunshots was still echoing around the dunes. Howard, who was more energetic than I'd have given him credit for, had called for help.

Three of us alive. Three of us dead. It was a horrible little scene.

"I didn't know Mirela had a gun," I complained.

He sounded amused. "Who do you think taught her to shoot?" he asked. "Who do you think got her a license? She's legal. She got her citizenship papers right before she left for Bulgaria."

"Have I mentioned lately that I really, really don't like you?" I asked.

"She thought she should be able to protect Lily," said Ali. "And Mirela being Mirela, she did something about it right away." Unlike *moi*: I'd have thought and thought and thought about "doing something" and finally would have done nothing. "I can't imagine she thought she'd have recourse to shooting this soon," Ali was saying. "Maybe later, when the boyfriends are lined up to date her…"

"Or girlfriends," I reminded him. "This is P'town."

"Do you know why she did it?" He wasn't talking about Mirela anymore.

"Yeah," I said. I could hear the sadness in my own voice. Billy had gotten Jordan a deal, a truly golden opportunity to go live in Los Angeles and do some recording—backup, some starring roles. Her voice had seduced everyone.

Eyes already set
on a land we never dreamed of
Moving closer every day

The problem had been Reggie. Reggie, who was committed to their community in ways that Jordan could only pretend to be. Reggie, who Jordan had only recently married, before they knew about the inheritance—Reggie, who by then had a say in how it would be spent. She wanted it to all go to her beloved charities. Jordan wanted to go to LA.

If they divorced, Reggie got half of everything.

"Mirela picked up on it when they were at the medical examiner's office," I told Ali. "Apparently they gave Jordan Reggie's effects, you know, what was on her when she—"

"I know what effects are," said Ali.

"Right. Well, there wasn't much, and it was all jewelry. A necklace, a watch, and a wedding ring. And on the way out, Jordan dropped the wedding ring in a rubbish container."

Mirela hadn't said anything, but she caught Jordan glancing at her in the car heading back. By the time they reached P'town, Jordan had made her decision to clear the decks.

Billy's price for getting rid of Reggie had been a percentage of the inheritance. He had hired Jed the bartender—who had the inside knowledge about Women's Week and the doctors in town—to help. He was dreaming of Beverly Hills and swimming pools and women in small bikinis.

He wasn't the brightest pixie in the forest. If Jordan were willing to kill her spouse rather than share the money, why on earth would she keep him—to her, an employee—around? Greed had blinded Billy, just as it had corrupted Jordan.

"I don't think Mirela would've gone into the dunes with Jordan if they'd been alone," I said to Ali.

"She had Lily with her," he said; I could feel him nodding.

"She had Lily with her," I agreed. I looked over to the temporary bassinet in which Lily was sleeping peacefully, her arms flung up over her head, blissfully unaware of how close she'd come to death. I wondered if we'd ever tell her. "So she didn't say anything. But Jordan was perceptive. She called Billy and Jed—they were the ones who actually did kill Reggie, because Jordan was paying Jed and promising Billy a career with her out in Los Angeles—and told them to meet her, and she stopped Mirela at Snail Road."

Howard had wasted no time. He couldn't find his phone, but Mirela's car was unlocked, and even though her phone wasn't, you can make 911 calls from a locked phone. Howard, it occurred to me, was a lot more enterprising than his mannerisms would have you believe.

"All it did was speed up what Jordan was going to do anyway. Meet Howard, sign the papers, making sure that it went into her account and not the ones he and Reggie had worked out. She was perfectly willing to threaten Howard if he didn't comply." I was relieved that it hadn't come to that; his heart might not have held out.

And it was such a beautiful, generous heart.

"What happens to him now?" Ali asked.

"He's going ahead with the reparations," I said. "This time, all of it going to those three places—Africville, the clinic, the church. And all as a memorial to Reggie." I sighed. "He has a cabin, he says." I couldn't imagine what kind of structure Howard would refer to as a cabin. "He's invited us to visit."

"Sounds like a plan, *cara*."

I sighed. Not anytime soon. For at least the next few weeks, I had a kid to take care of. I also had bridges to mend back at the inn, where Mike had been compelled to cover both my weddings, probably swearing a blue streak at my unexplained absence. I still had another wedding coming up on Saturday. Impossible as it was to believe, Women's Week wasn't even over yet. I still had so much to do. It would be a really bad time to go away, especially with a baby in tow. A really bad time.

"Hey," I said to Ali. "You want some company?"

Author's Note

As usual, I've taken one or two liberties with reality.

There really was a ship captain called William Dutton, but he didn't build the Race Point Inn; he built a lovely house out in North Truro and is buried in the cemetery on Route Six. (I imagine that means that in the end he made it safely home.) I lived in the real William Dutton House for many years, and on windy nights I imagined his family clustered around the stove, hoping he'd make it back from sea. I loved that house, and I thought a lot about him, too, the captain, weary of lonely nights shared by stars and moon glinting whitely on water, aching for floors that didn't move under his feet. I wanted to honor him here.

I've moved a few rooms around out at the Provincetown Inn and added in a coat closet or two, but by and large it's how I describe it here. It's a marvelous taste of the atmosphere Provincetown used to have and is rapidly losing, so by all means if you visit, go out and stroll through the place.

The Underground Railroad did indeed have a terminus in Provincetown, and there's evidence that at least three houses (the Martin House, the Ryder home—moved for the construction of Town Hall—and the Stephen Nickerson home in the West End) were used to shelter fugitives before the time was right for them to go out to sea and be spirited away to Nova Scotia.

Captain Stephen Nickerson, a member of King Hiram's Lodge, is said to have been one of the wealthiest men in Provincetown when "vessel property was good property." He owned the 188-ton bark Spartan, *engaging another member of the Lodge, Josiah Cook, as captain. His home at 54 Commercial Street is known as the 1807 House. During the Civil War his home was one of four houses in Provincetown functioning as part of the Underground Railway System. Black slaves escaping north to Canada found food and shelter at these stations during the day. At night they were boarded onto fishing schooners leaving Provincetown for the Grand Banks and the Maritime Provinces." (James Theriault,* Every First Monday)

I learned about this from Julia Perry, current chair of the Provincetown Historical Association and a member of the History Project, who's writing a book about the Underground Railroad in Provincetown. Julia did a talk at a Women's Week event *last* year, and I started writing this book that very night, I was so inspired and energized by our history.

There was in fact an Africville in Halifax, and its community and destruction are pretty much as I describe. Look it up; the story is heartbreaking.

In case it isn't clear, mooncussers were essentially shore-pirates. On dark nights, they'd demolish lighthouses and erect decoy signals to entice ships onto the dangerous shoals of the Cape; when the ship wrecked, they'd plunder it. The word came about because they cursed the moon when it was bright, which gave sailors more opportunity to see where they were going and possibly save themselves.

Only one of the disappearances with which this story began actually happened. While the slave Sarah is my invention, Dorothy May Bradford was very real. It is impossible for me to believe that she "slipped" off the deck of the Mayflower when it was peacefully at anchor in the harbor, though that is the official story. Some believe she jumped. Some believe she was pushed. I don't think we'll ever know. Her husband went on to become the first governor of the Commonwealth of Massachusetts; we have both a street and a bar/restaurant here in Provincetown named for him.

Finally, I want to let first-time Sydney Riley readers know that P'town is actually not a murder (or suicide) capital of anywhere: our crime waves tend to involve the borrowing and/or theft of bicycles. All the violence and mayhem in this and every other Provincetown mystery is entirely of my own making.

Come visit: I promise you won't get bumped off!

Acknowledgments

As always, first, last, and foremost, my gratitude goes to Arthur Mahoney of HomePort Press. Sydney belongs to him as much as she does to me. He is a friend, colleague, guru, and all-around delight. I wish every author had an Arthur Mahoney in their life.

And again as always I need to thank all the beautiful people of Provincetown, who generously allow me to use so many of their own special selves in my books. Any errors in their portrayal are mine.

To those who contribute in myriad ways to the creation of a Sydney story: Colin Kegler, Amanda Robinson, Susan Blood, Pat Medina, Cathy Knipper, Chip Capelli, Robin Fredey, Ann Robinson, Michael Ponestowski, Freddy Biddle, Carem Bennett, Dianne Kopser, Michelle Crone (whose wedding planning inspires Sydney, and who first suggested this series), Bob Allen, Julie and Katy Blackburn, Lady Di, and Tony, Suzanne, and Albert Rodrigues. Thank you to my beautiful family, Anastasia, Jacob, and Sydnia Czarnecki; and to

Sister Kathryn, for always inspiring me to do and be better.

Thanks to Deborah Karacozian, Nan Cinnater, and Clayton Nottleman for being my emissaries at the Provincetown Bookshop, to Jeff Peters and East End Books—as well as to Amy Raff and Brittany Taylor of the Provincetown Public Library—for fabulous book launch parties, and to Miladinka Milic for Sydney's amazing cover designs.

Thanks to Erin Delaney for editing, and to my wonderful First Readers: Kimberlee Sams, Corinne Diana, Margo Nash, Deborah Karacozian (again!), and A.C. Burch. Any mistakes that remain here are mine, not theirs.

My gratitude goes out to you all, to all of my beautiful seaside home, and to anyone I might have inadvertently left out—for sometimes I am a bear of very little brain.

No, not that kind of bear.

About the Author

Jeannette de Beauvoir writes mystery and historical fiction (and often books at the intersection of the two) that uncover dark secrets and hidden truths, and explore a sense of connection to place.

A Book Sense Book-of-the-Year finalist, she's a member of the Authors Guild, the Mystery Writers of America, Sisters in Crime, and the National Writers Union.

Her delight is to find characters true to the spaces in which they live. She herself lives and writes in a cottage in Provincetown, on Cape Cod, Massachusetts, and loves the collection of people who assemble at a place like Land's End.

Find out more at:
jeannettedebeauvoir.com.

Did You Enjoy This Book?

If you did, please…

1) **share your opinion** on Goodreads and/or Amazon;

2) **visit my Amazon page** and check out some of my other books;

3) give the book a boost; **tell people about** it on Facebook and Twitter;

4) **subscribe to my newsletter** at **jeannettedebeauvoir.com** for book reviews, short stories, quizzes, free stuff, previews of upcoming work, and more;

5) ask your local bookseller **to stock** Sydney Riley books;

6) make them your **choice for your next book club** meeting (I'll even join you by Skype or Zoom if you'd like me to!);

7) **email me** at jeannettedebeauvoir@gmail.com;

8) and **watch for** the next Sydney Riley mystery from Homeport Press!